DEAR CHRISTMAS

SARAH READY

W|W
CROWN

ALSO BY SARAH READY

Stand Alone Romances:

The Fall in Love Checklist

Hero Ever After

Once Upon an Island

French Holiday

The Space Between

The Ghosted Series:

Ghosted

Switched

Josh and Gemma:

Josh and Gemma Make a Baby

Josh and Gemma the Second Time Around

Soul Mates in Romeo Romance Series:

Chasing Romeo

Love Not at First Sight

Romance by the Book

Love, Artifacts, and You

Married by Sunday

My Better Life

Scrooging Christmas

Stand Alone Novella:

Love Letters

Find these books and more by Sarah Ready at:

www.sarahready.com/romance-books

WHAT WOULD YOU DO IF YOU RECEIVED A CHRISTMAS CARD FROM SOMEONE YOU'VE NEVER MET?

When Cordelia Hobday receives a surprise Christmas card from a stranger—the funny, kind, and interesting Lee Weston—she decides to write him back.

But there are rules to this Christmas letter exchange:

They'll never meet.

They'll never call.

They'll never email.

They'll save a year's worth of wishes and secrets, hopes and dreams, and share them every Christmas in one *Dear Christmas* letter.

They'll be friends for life.

And the most important rule of all? They will never, ever, ever fall in love.

Ten years of Christmases. Ten years of letters. One Christmas wish...

This is a Soul Mates in Romeo Christmas Novel.

Dear Christmas

SARAH READY

CROWN

W.W. CROWN BOOKS
An imprint of Swift & Lewis Publishing LLC
www.wwcrown.com

Library of Congress Control Number: 2023949261
ISBN: 978-1-954007-72-7 (eBook)
ISBN: 978-1-954007-73-4 (pbk)
ISBN: 978-1-954007-74-1 (large print)
ISBN: 978-1-954007-75-8 (hbk)

A quick letter from Sarah...

Merry Christmas!

This book is the best of two worlds—romance and Christmas. Last year, I wrote a book about a grumpy Scrooge named Gabe in *Scrooging Christmas*. His brother Lee had been missing for more than twenty years. This book is Lee's story.

When I wrote *Dear Christmas*, I'd been thinking about Christmas letters. Do you receive letters in the mail at Christmastime? Isn't it fun how when someone writes a letter their voice is so present you can practically hear them speaking out loud? Christmas letters have always been a way to connect people.

Thinking about letters, I wondered what would happen if two people who never met wrote Christmas letters to each other and shared all their secrets?

Dear Christmas is written in letter form with Lee and Cordelia exchanging Christmas letters every year. I hope you can hear both Lee's and Cordelia's voices strong and clear through their own words.

Lee has a fondness for dropping commas, adding extra commas, and stringing independent clauses together into Christmas garland length run-on sentences. You'll notice his letters wouldn't pass a grammar check. But if I'd tidied him up and chopped his run-ons into two or three sentences then he wouldn't be Lee. He's quiet, thoughtful, and humble and his sentences and paragraphs are long, cozy, and warm.

Meanwhile, Cordelia is more direct. Her sentences are short. Her paragraphs are small. She rarely uses a comma when a period works just as well. She has a sense of humor and an appreciation for life. She's warm-hearted, has a fondness for honesty, and like Lee says, "She'll be your friend for life."

I hope you love reading *Dear Christmas* and watching Lee and Cordelia fall in love.

Merry Christmas!

All the best,
    Sarah

Dear Christmas

PROLOGUE

Dear Lee,

I know this Christmas card will never reach you.

I know these words will never find you.

I know each word I write pulls me further away from you. As if each letter is another beat in time, pushing us apart.

But if I could have one Christmas wish come true, it would be you.

Somehow, the Christmas cards I wrote became pieces of my soul addressed to you. I didn't mean to love you, but that's what happened.

I love you.

I need you.

Please.

I need you.

If somehow this letter can fly off the page and find its way to your heart—

I need you.
Find me in Romeo. Find me at Christmas.

Yours,
Cordelia

Return To Sender ->
January 12
Postage Due

ten years ago

1

Cordelia Hobday
   1621 Tenderfoot Lane
   Romeo, NY

Dear Cordelia,

Merry Christmas. The lady here told me that if I wrote you a Christmas card it'd make you feel better. She said you just had heart surgery and if I wrote you then you wouldn't feel so terrible about being shut up in your house, not able to come to the Christmas Market. Well, I don't know anything about heart surgery. I guess I'd just be glad to be alive and not complain so much about missing a bunch of people crowded together buying fake wreaths and ugly ornaments carved from cheap wood, but that's just me.

But the lady said you were sad and I was the only one who could cheer you up. In an effort to be completely honest, I'm only writing because she promised ten dollars if I did.

She said you are one of a kind. The sort of person who I could write to and tell anything, the sort of person who I could count on to stick around in bad times and good. She said if I wrote you, you'd be my friend for your whole life.

Not to be rude, but I'm not sure you have too long to live considering you're friends with a lady who looks about 900 years old and you just had heart surgery yourself.

But I'm willing to take a chance on this letter because I need the money. I'm making my way up to Prince Edward Island. I've got a job there this winter working construction, but I don't have enough money to make it up there just yet. I could hitch hike, but I sort of got turned off that last summer when some nut almost slit my throat one night for the bag of Fritos in my cargo pants' pocket.

I guess you don't want to hear about that. Anyway, I'm not especially into Christmas. Sometimes, I remember Christmas with my family. My brother and my parents. But I think, probably those are just false memories. I bet someday, I'll see a made for TV Christmas movie playing at a bus stop, and there'll be my memory mom and dad, and my memory big brother right there on the TV screen acting out my one Christmas memory.

The only thing I ever had to prove it was real was this little ornament, but I sold it today. I remember my brother saying it was a Christmas magic ornament, but if that were true, if I had a brother, then wouldn't I be with him? Wouldn't I be with that family I sort of, almost remember?

You might be getting worried for me. Don't. I'm alright. I'm fourteen now and taller than most anybody and I have these brown-black eyes and black hair that make me look meaner and older than I am, so nobody much bothers me. Plus, I have an ID that says I'm eighteen, and everyone believes it. Besides, when you travel around as much as I do you meet a lot of people, and most of them are decent. I guess I get by on the small kindnesses of strangers.

Maybe that's why I'm writing you. Small kindnesses. Although, I'm still taking the ten dollars.

But please take care of yourself. And get better. Take it easy, don't get out of bed too soon, and watch as many cheesy Christmas movies as you like. You could also try Campbell's Chicken Noodle Soup—that's what I get from the store when I'm not feeling well. You can drink it from the can if you're too tired to heat it up. I do that sometimes. It still tastes fine.

It'd be nice if you didn't die because I've never written a Christmas letter to anyone before and it'd be sad if the first person I wrote to died before she could write back.

Also, since you're sad that you can't be at the Christmas Market I'll describe it to you so that later you can close your eyes and pretend you're here.

The table I'm sitting at is near the cider and hot cocoa stand. It's a little red hut with Christmas lights and the smell of cinnamon and apple and melted chocolate is so strong that my eyes nearly water from it. The man there, he has this big beard that takes up half his face, gave me a huge Styrofoam cup of cider with a cinnamon stick and orange slices and cranberries floating in it. The cup was so hot that it burned my fingers. I wanted to drink it fast because I've been sitting out here for hours, and I haven't eaten since last night, and I'm so cold I can't remember what warm feels like, but I've just been drinking it for the past hour, taking these tiny sips because it tastes like, well, have you ever been outside this town?

Maybe you've been up north, where the cedar and pine stretch for miles and there isn't anyone out there, just you and snow and silence. But then, when you're sitting on the side of the road, snow mounds so high, the sun melting the snow so it falls off the pine branches and slides to the ground, and your breath comes out in front of you crystallizing in a fog, and then a deer steps out of the cedars and stares at you before bounding off. That deer makes you remember you aren't alone. It makes you glad to be alive in a world where you aren't alone. That's what this cider tastes like.

So there's music playing at the Christmas Market too. It's cranked over the speakers, kind of crackly like it's playing on a tape deck from four decades ago. It's the classics. Burl Ives, Bing Crosby, Nat King Cole (I rode with a trucker once who loved those guys). And I guess if they played them anywhere, this is where they'd fit.

Romeo, your town, is all covered in snow and ice so that the buildings look like frosted gingerbread houses. There are candy cane ribbons wrapped around the street lights and Christmas lights strung on all the buildings. There are Christmas trees stacked in the tree lot—blue spruce, Fraser fir, white pine—they smell like evergreen, the good, fresh kind, not the air freshener kind, and about fifteen different families have hauled a tree away since I've been here.

The entire street is lined with painted wooden huts and tables. There's a make your own wreath booth, a make your own snow globe hut, a gingerbread decorating table, tables with ornaments, Christmas cards, photos with Santa and the elves. There are even reindeer. Three of them. I have to admit, I pet one. I was walking past and he leaned over and stole my mitten from my jacket pocket. I pulled it out of his mouth then put my hand on his nose. It was wet and soft, soft like the velvet on one of those velvet posters you can buy in travel rest stops. When I spread my fingers on his nose, he let out a breath, it fogged up the air and smelled sweet like dried clover. I pet him until he tried to nibble my jacket, then I went and set up my table.

I'm selling those cheap wood ornaments I told you about. I learned to carve from this army vet in Poughkeepsie. I spent all last month making them. My fingers are all nicked up and sore, but I have fifty trees, stars, and Christmas hearts, and by tonight I'll have enough money to make it up north.

I figure, since you can't be here, I'll send an ornament with this letter. It's a Christmas heart. I'm only sending it because if your heart is broken, or still mending, then maybe this one can be a substitute until yours gets better.

The lady says you'll write back, but if you don't that's alright. I'm not looking for a friend, I'm just looking for ten dollars. And since I got that, I guess we're even.

But I'll wait around and not catch the bus until morning. Just because, I guess, I want to know that you'll be alright. I feel, sort of like I know you already, even if you haven't written back yet. I guess, when the lady said you've been through a lot in your life and you'd understand anything I had to say, I guess, it made me hopeful.

I hope you have a happy Christmas.

—Lee Weston

~

Lee Weston
    c/o Erma Tanaka
    Christmas Market
    Cheap Wood Ornament Table
    Romeo, NY

Dear Lee,

Merry Christmas. Joyeux Noël. Feliz Navidad. Buon Natale. Frohe Weihnachten.

I want to reassure you. I'm not dead. I'm not even half-dead or a quarter-dead. During surgery, my heart stopped, but they restarted it right away. So I can't even claim that I was (once) an eighth or a sixteenth dead.

If I was, I'd like to come back as a Christmas ghost. Like Marley. I'd haunt Romeo and pop out of chimneys and shout, "Boo, only coal for you!" Or I'd stick my ghostly head out of fruit cakes and pretend to gag. Because, Lee, I despise fruit cake. Despise it.

Why is it that people still insist on making fruit cake, even though the only people who like fruit cake are jaywalkers and serial killers? It's one of the modern world's greatest mysteries.

Did you know, when people say, "not to be rude," you can be sure that whatever they are about to say is incredibly rude. What's wrong with having a bum heart? It's all fixed now. And what's wrong with having Miss Erma as a friend? She was in the hospital getting a new knee last year while I was there for my second heart surgery (this one was my third, and my last, I promise).

At the retirement home, I love to play bridge and cribbage. We drink chamomile tea and eat these little almond cookies with raspberry jam. I go on weekends. Otherwise, I live on Tenderfoot Lane in the blue and yellow Victorian with the pink shutters and the wraparound porch. It looks like a giant frilly doily. Or a wobbly wedding cake if you squint and cross your eyes.

Anyway, if you haven't realized yet that people who look 900 years old are a hundred times more interesting than practically anyone else in the world, then I think you need to give them a chance. You seem like someone who is open to new experiences.

By the way, I agree with you. It's probably best that you don't hitchhike in New York. If you continue that practice you will probably end up dead before me. Then I'd be the one with a Christmas pen pal who died before his time.

We are pen pals, aren't we? I can't pay you. So you'll have to write me for another reason. I'd like to suggest one.

It sounds like you don't have a family. I'm not being mean, just pragmatic. I'm not sure you have friends either. Not good ones at least, if you're fourteen and writing a stranger for ten dollars. If you had good friends, you probably wouldn't be in this situation.

I'm not going to offend you by offering you a place to stay. Well, if you like, you're welcome to stay at my house. The attic is big, clean, and warm. Even in winter. Although in summer it's an oven. There's also the trouble with what everyone would think, me keeping a mean looking boy in my attic. But what's life without a little eccentricity? I'm joking. I wouldn't keep you in my attic. There's a guest room with ugly paisley wallpaper that you could stay in.

But I get the feeling that you're set on Prince Edward Island. If that's the case, here's my reason for us writing each other.

You don't have anyone.

And me, I have a lot of someones. My life is so full of someones that sometimes I can't get a breath. I'm not complaining. It's just . . . they're all so scared for me. Their worry is as heavy as those chains Marley dragged around. What does that mean? It means I don't have anyone to talk to. Out of a hundred people, I don't have one who I can tell . . . I'm terrified I'm going to die.

Not that I'm terrified of death. I'm terrified I'm going to die.

There was a story in *The Reader's Digest*. I read it in my cardiologist's waiting room. It was this tale about a dog whose owner died, and it visited the owner's grave for eight years, every day, until it died too. It was supposed to be sweet. Sweet! But that story terrified me. Is that what I'd leave behind? If I die, will I leave behind a dog that can't let go? That's a metaphor for my family in case you didn't catch it.

But I *can't* tell anyone that. It would just hurt them. So I act brave. Happy. Patient. I don't bother anyone or ask for anything.

Right now, I'm asking for something. Because you're a stranger and you couldn't (really) care less whether or not I die. Or whether or not I'm scared. Or tired, or angry, or selfish. I don't have to worry about hurting you by being afraid.

And you can do the same.

I bet, not remembering your family, not knowing where you're going to get your next ten dollars from, I bet that's scary. And I bet you can't admit it to anyone.

Maybe not even yourself.

So how about, we write to each other. How about we send Christmas cards every year, and we tell each other all the things we can't even tell ourselves. We can save up a year's worth of truths and share them.

I'll tell you one now:

Sometimes I wish that I could run away. Far, far away. Because for years my world has been dominated by the four walls of a hospital room. I'd like to run somewhere where there aren't any walls.

Write me back? Before you leave Romeo? It doesn't have to be a long letter. Just a yes or a no, to let me know whether you'll send me a card next year, with an address I can write to.

Yours,
    Cordelia

P.S. Thank you for writing about the Christmas Market. I really wanted to go. I can almost taste the hot cider. The hungry reindeer's name is Clyde and he has stolen more mittens than I can count. Also, thank you for the ornament. I think it's the prettiest ornament I've ever seen. Even if the wood is cheap. I'll hang it on my bedpost and look at it before I fall asleep. Oh, I forgot. I don't know if your memories are real or not, but I do think there is still Christmas magic. Write back.

P.P.S. I enclosed my lucky penny. I don't need it anymore, so I'm giving it to you. It's kept me alive for three surgeries. Since you sold your Christmas magic ornament, you can have this to replace it. Keep it in your pocket. It still has some magic left.

P.P.P.S. I forgot. Rules! If we're going to be Christmas pen pals saving up all our secrets and truths then there has to be rules. One, we only write letters because email, phone, whatever, that's not the same. There's something about the lead of pencil against paper that lets you share things you never would otherwise. Two, we stay strangers in real life. Sometimes it feels safer to tell your vulnerabilities to a stranger, don't you agree? Three, no photos. Let's stay words on a page, just Christmas cards, okay?

~

Cordelia Hobday
    1621 Tenderfoot Lane
    Romeo, NY

Dear Cordelia,

Yes.

—Lee

P.S. I'm glad you're not dead. Thanks for the housing offer, but no thanks. I'm better on my own. I'll write you next Christmas. I hope your heart is better by then. One last thing. I love fruit cake. I'm not a serial killer, but I do jaywalk. All the time. I guess that proves your point. Anyway, I guess we're friends now. Thank you for the penny, I promise to keep it with me.

nine years ago

2

———————

NINE YEARS AGO

Cordelia Hobday
   1621 Tenderfoot Lane
   Romeo, NY

Dear Cordelia,

Merry Christmas. I have to be honest, I almost didn't send this letter. First, it's been a whole year, and a lot has happened, and you were just one letter (two, I guess), fifteen minutes out of a whole year. But then I got thinking, which Jackson tells me I do too much, and I started feeling guilty because I said I'd write you, didn't I? I don't have much in this world, but three years ago, when this old lady dropped a wad of cash (like five hundred dollars) outside her car at a gas station, I picked it up and ran after her and gave it to her. And she looked at me and said, "You sure have integrity."

I looked it up at the next library I stopped at. Having integrity means being honest and moral, even when no one is looking. I liked that. A person can be stripped of money, or their home, or their family, but nothing can make you lose your integrity. So I decided that I'd always have integrity. I guess that's why I'm writing you. I said I would, so here I am.

I'm not sure you'll write back. I've been wondering lately if you're still alive. I know you told me you weren't planning on dying, but hearts give out and people die all the time. Are you still scared of that, not of dying, but of leaving your family behind? Are you still weighed down by their worry?

I didn't say this last year, but I've had time to think about it. I'm sort of envious of you. You might be kicking up your heels, pushing up the daisies, croaking and landing in a pine box, but at least you have a family that cares. You'd probably have a funeral full of weeping people. I bet you don't know how lucky that is. I'd give just about anything to have just one person care. Heck, to have one person <u>notice</u> that I'm dying. Sometimes I wonder if it's possible to live an entire life without a single person noticing that you've done so. A lot of times, I feel like that ghost you mentioned. I pass through towns, walk in and out of people's lives, and most times I don't think anybody sees me.

Jackson tells me I need to quit thinking so much. He says a nineteen year old (he doesn't know I'm fifteen) should only be thinking about beers, girls, and nuthin' else. I guess I'll tell you about Jackson and his brother, Saul.

Back last December I made it up to Prince Edward Island, but it turned out the construction job wasn't, well, it wasn't happening anymore. Okay. I'll be honest. Like you said, we're supposed to tell each other things we wouldn't even tell ourselves. Since I don't want to tell myself this and I don't like to think about it, I guess I'll tell you.

The construction job was real. It was tearing down this big old brick building and I was set to do removal work. I showed up and found the boss, started that day and then after work all the guys went down to the bar. They dragged me along and before I knew it one of the guys had lost his wallet. I guess you know where this is going.

It was eight guys. All of them knew each other for years, and none of them knew me. So in no time I was in the parking lot, getting the, excuse my language, shit kicked out of me for stealing Boomer's ninety three dollars, his hunting and fishing license, and his coffee club stamp card. I know you don't have any reason to believe I didn't do it, especially because two days before I'd written you a letter for ten dollars, except for what I told you about integrity. Maybe you could believe I have integrity.

So anyway, I got a broken nose, a chipped tooth, busted knuckles, a lump on my head the size of a grapefruit, and a couple broken ribs. At least, I think they were broken. I didn't go to the doctor. My knuckles were busted up because I fought back. Not that one kid can do much against eight guys.

Anyway, I passed out in the snowbank outside that crappy bar with beer posters blocking the light in the windows and all the cars cold, and nobody coming in or out of the bar to find me. It was cold out, that kind where the air freezes in your lungs and sucks all the moisture out. The cold where your eyeballs feel like solid chunks of ice and your blood is freezing in your veins. You know what I mean? So I guess I didn't feel the cold though. I was just sort of floating there, in and out of consciousness.

And this is the part I don't like to think about. I kept seeing that Christmas I remember, that maybe false memory when I had a family.

I'm in this big city, I think it's New York, because it looks just like all those Christmas movies you see where they're set in New York. And I'm in front of this massive Christmas tree. It's as tall as a skyscraper, and I look up and up and up. It's beautiful. My memory mom is there, and my dad, and I'm holding my memory brother's hand. In my other, I have my ornament. My brother says, "Look at it, Lee! Look at the lights!"

Then this is where it gets weird. Instead of looking at the tree, I look around. I'm surrounded by hundreds, maybe thousands of people, and they're all in winter coats and mittens and hats, but none of them have faces. It's all these people and none of them have faces. They're just flat, blank surfaces. No eyes, no mouths, nothing.

Then I realize my brother is gone. So are my mom and dad.

I was lying in that snowbank, I don't know how long, drifting between an ice cold snowbank and running through New York trying to find my family. Then all that disappeared and it was just me in the snow, frostbitten and probably dying. Here's what scares me. Here's why I don't like to think about it. I got warm all of a sudden. I stopped feeling the freezing cold and the pain in my head and I just let go. Like I let go of my memory brother's hand.

I guess maybe I was going to die. Maybe I shouldn't have been worried about you dying. Maybe I should've been worried about me.

It scared me, much later, because I realized that the only person who would care or notice if I died, was me. And at that moment, even I didn't care.

But anyway, I didn't die. Instead, this bright light hit me. It looked a lot like that tunnel light people always talk about before they fly up to heaven. But it was just Jackson in his Ford F-150.

He pulled over, hauled me into his truck, and swore at me and knocked me around until I fully woke up. I guess, if you couldn't tell, Jackson doesn't believe in coddling.

Anyway, he took me to his and Saul's place, up north in New Brunswick. They're brothers, and they live up in the middle of nowhere, in this log cabin they built fifty years ago. I guess they're what you'd call hermits. Not spiritual or philosophical or anything like that, they just don't like people much. I don't know why Jackson pulled me in his truck that night. He doesn't either. I asked him once, and he said, it was the same as pulling a fox out of a trap and shooting it. You don't want it to suffer. You just kill it quick. I guess him rescuing me was putting me out of my misery.

I've been with Jackson and Saul a full year now. It's different from anything I've ever had before. Mainly because I've never stayed in one place this long in my whole life. Even when I was six or seven, I was on the move, avoiding the type of people you learn real quick to avoid.

If you didn't know, I'm talking about the bad sorts and the do-gooders, they're about the same to a kid like me. In fact, sometimes the bad sorts were better because at least they were honest about their intentions. I'm not especially fond of do-gooders. If you take one sprinkle of help, they think they're entitled to tell you what to do, where to be, they think they own your life. I've been on my own too much to let anyone own me or feel entitled to me. That's why I don't mind Jackson and Saul.

Neither of them talk much. Jackson doesn't talk because he's gruff and angry and had a hard time of it, I guess. I think, with him, he has too much to say, so he doesn't say anything at all. It gets that way sometimes. A body can have so many words crammed inside them that they get all clogged up and then nothing can come out.

Saul doesn't talk either. But he says he doesn't talk because he ran out of things to say about thirty years ago. He said once you've lived long enough you realize people are just saying the same things over and over again, and you realize, so are you. He didn't want to be part of the problem so he just stopped talking. Saul isn't angry. He's just Saul.

Sometimes I'll talk, just to break the silence. But I only do when I think it's something important to say, like, "Thank you for taking me in." Jackson will grunt at that and Saul will pat my arm. "We're almost out of meat." To which Jackson will toss me a rifle or a fishing pole. So I stopped saying that one, and just got the fishing pole when I needed to. Or, "Do you believe in God?" Neither of them said anything to that one. Sometimes, when we're out in the woods, cutting wood for our cord deliveries, I'll just talk, wondering and thinking, and then Jackson will say, "You think too much. Quit thinking so much."

Anyway, the cabin is built from pine logs and it has this golden, wild honey color that gets richer when the afternoon sun streams through the fir trees. The cabin was built with care, but also with economy, so it's rectangular, one story, eight hundred square feet, with only two windows, a wood stove, and a small kitchen. The toilet (just a deep hole, really) and washing tub are in a shed outside. I guess, fifty years ago, Jackson and Saul weren't thinking about how tromping through the snow when it's below freezing just to take a, excuse my language, piss, would be a real pain in the butt.

I do the laundry, and even in winter, I hang it on the line between two fir trees. The wet clothes freeze first, they get all crunchy and ice covered, then because there isn't any moisture in the air, all that ice gets sucked up when the sun comes out. If you hang a pair of pants out in the morning, they'll be dry by dinner. Freezing cold, but mostly dry.

Inside, the bedrooms are separated by sheets hung from the ceiling. I don't have a bed, but I do have a little cozy curtained-off space. I laid old coveralls and winter coats on the floor and bunched them together to make a mattress. I have a few books, although I'm not much of a reader because people in books always seem whiny to me. Or they're in self-denial which is nearly as bad. I just can't seem to relate to them. I've got your Christmas card though. I liked the cardinals on the front, so I set it on the little wooden shelf against the wall and sometimes I look at it as the light fades and the logs crack and hiss in the woodstove.

The cabin always smells like burning wood and aged pine. Sometimes it smells like venison, or duck, maybe trout. But usually, it's smoke that fills the air. I think the smoke has permeated my skin, so that even a hundred years from now I'll still smell like it.

You might be wondering what it's like here? I'll tell you. It's quiet. It's quiet inside the cabin and it's quiet outside too. We're miles deep, down an old dirt road, and then miles more down a rutted grass road cut through a balsam fir forest. Somedays the quiet is so deep, it's hard to believe that there are any people living in the world at all. There are white tailed deer here, they're my favorite, because of how they pause in the shadow of the trees and look at you with this solemn, wide stare, like they are looking at something inside you that even you can't see. There are snowshoe hare, with these thick, warm white coats that you want to bury your nose in and just breathe in. You can't see them, except for the fact that when they run, it looks like the snow is moving in a blur. Saul has a pair of leather mittens lined with their fur and sometimes he lets me wear them, especially when I'm out for hours hauling wood. You'd think I might feel conflicted, liking the hare running past, but also using them to keep my hands warm. I don't though. Being conflicted about keeping warm is a particular luxury I've not gotten the privilege to experience yet. Maybe someday I will. Which I suppose would be nice.

Anyway, I could tell you about the black bear that tries to steal our garbage, or the mated pair of coyotes all gray and silver and brown that live in a den not far from the cabin, or I could even tell you about the day I ran into a skunk, and Saul had to dump a gallon of tinned tomato juice on me, but I won't.

It's been a long, quiet, lonely year. I won't kid myself to think that Jackson and Saul care about me. They're nearing eighty. They make money by cutting down trees, curing the wood, and delivering cords in their truck to all the wood burning folks within a hundred miles. I do most the work now. Not because they asked, but because . . . I suppose, because of that thing called integrity. Not to put it too strongly, but Jackson saved my life, even though he was a stranger at the time. I can't repay him. But I can cut wood, deliver cords, make sure their freezer is full of venison and fish. I think, if I left tomorrow, they wouldn't mind, maybe they wouldn't even notice for a few days that I'd gone.

Do you remember that story you told about the dog visiting its owner's grave for years after they died? Well maybe I'm that dog. I'm staying in this old cabin with two old guys who don't have any use for me, who don't speak to me, who don't much care. They're like that grave, all silent and cold, and I'm that dog that keeps hanging around.

I guess I do think too much.

But Cordelia. There. Maybe you thought I'd forgotten that I'm writing to you, not just a piece of paper that can't write back. Cordelia, do you think, maybe, do you think things get better, or do you think they just get different?

Never mind, don't answer that. I'd erase it, but this pencil doesn't have an eraser and I don't have enough paper to start again. That old lady at the Christmas Market said you were the kind of person who understands and doesn't judge. I like that about you. I hope it's true. I think it is.

Jackson and Saul don't celebrate Christmas. I might cook venison and potatoes, but maybe not. I think, it'll be quiet. Lonely. I don't think anyone will say Merry Christmas out loud. Only me. So this year, if you write back, you'll be the only person to say Merry Christmas to me.

I hope you do. When I started this letter, I told myself I didn't care whether or not you wrote back. But now, my hand's shaking a bit, and my chest is tight, like it is when the chimney's blocked and the smoke from the wood stove is too thick, and I guess, I care. I care a lot. Please write back.

Tell me what Christmas is like in Romeo. Tell me about your life, where your wedding cake house is filled with your always worrying family. A huge, lit up tree surrounded by presents. A feast on the table. Carolers and hot cocoa. A Christmas like in one of those movies. I never had a Christmas like that, not one I can remember. One of those with joy and laughter. Will you please write and describe it for me so I can pretend on Christmas Day that I'm there too? Even if no one notices me, I'd like to pretend that I'm there in a Christmas like that. At least for a day. There, that's something I never thought I'd admit.

I hope you are well. I hope you are healthy. I hope your heart is fixed. I hope you have a Merry Christmas. I'll write again next year if you're still alive. I hope you're still alive.

Merry Christmas, Cordelia.

—Lee

P.S. I included balsam fir needles from the woods near the cabin so that you can close your eyes, breathe in, and pretend you are here. Also, I guess maybe your penny really was lucky, since Jackson found me and I didn't die, so I always keep it in my pocket, just in case.

Lee Weston
12933 E. Beaver Lake Road
Stalwart Branch, NB
Canada

Dear Lee,

Did you know, I haven't had to assure anyone of my vital signs in at least eight hours. You will be gratified to know that I'm still upright, respirating, and haven't yet ascended to the great beyond. The daisies will have to push themselves up without me. For many, many years, I promise you.

Now that that is out of the way. Hello. Hi. Oh, hi!

I'm glad you wrote. More than glad. I'm going to admit that when I received your Christmas card, I ran (more like slipped down the icy sidewalk at a running pace) into the house, clasped the envelope to my chest, and laughed out loud. I haven't felt so exhilarated in a long time.

I won't lie and pretend not to know why. It's because for the past year, off and on, I've thought of you. I've worried for you. Let me tell you. That is a new experience. Usually I'm the one on the receiving end of worry. But I worried.

There was a large blank canvas where knowledge of your life hung. You were living (I thought), working (I thought), traveling (I thought). But I didn't know.

I have to admit, I built a million stories around you. They were ridiculous stories. Very melodramatic. Sometimes you were attacked by rabid wild dogs. Other times you fell off a roof on the job. You broke your leg or something like that. Other times you had your throat slit because you hitchhiked again and had a bag of Doritos in your pocket (which, let's admit, are much more dangerous than Fritos).

Other times you won the lottery, three hundred million dollars. You bought a mansion, a Ferrari, and a kangaroo. And I'd never know because after becoming a multimillionaire, you wouldn't need to write me anymore. (Don't mind the kangaroo bit. I only included that in my fantasy because I'd just finished a non-fiction book where this aristocrat had a menagerie at his estate, including kangaroos).

But you wrote me. You wrote me! I'm happier about that than I have a right to be.

So let me be the first to tell you, and let me say it with as much enthusiasm, cheer, and heartfelt good wishes as I can—

MERRY CHRISTMAS!

There. How was that? It didn't feel like it was enough. I shouted it, but I'm not sure it reached through New York, Vermont, New Hampshire, Maine, and New Brunswick to reach you up in those thick, silent, balsam fir woods.

So I'll try again. Here, I'm holding out my hands.

They're still a bit cold from my walk outside when I found your letter in the mailbox. Take them. Hold them in yours, which I imagine are warm from your fur-lined mittens. (By the way, I can feel guilty for you in regard to the snowshoe hare. I'm Catholic and we're spoon-fed guilt with our Wheaties so that we can grow up big and strong).

Okay, take my hands. Take a step closer. Lean down. If you're as tall as I think, then I probably only come up to your shoulders. So lean down. Now look in my eyes.

They're green, by the way.

You can picture them because they are the green of the balsam fir needles you sent. Look into my eyes, I'm smiling. I smell like peppermint and chocolate, because I just drank hot cocoa and used a candy cane to stir it. It's chilly inside, because this is an old, drafty Victorian, and the fire place looks pretty, but it couldn't heat a closet. Now squeeze my hands.

And listen.

Merry Christmas, Lee. Merry Christmas.

You wondered if anyone would notice if you're gone. I'd notice.

I know in the grand scheme of things, I'm not very important. You've never met me. You don't know me. I'm just someone you wrote a Christmas card to once. Well, twice.

But, Lee, I spent a good part of the last year imagining you either slaughtered by the Doritos serial killer or lounging in your million-dollar mansion with your pet kangaroo. So I'm invested.

I've confided in you this past year, even if I didn't write it down. I saved up all my truths, carrying them for you. The funny thing is, by holding them for you, I was able to let them go. Just the thought of being able to tell it all to you in a letter made me not need to tell it at all.

Not everyone can say that they have someone like you.

So, I'd notice. My life would be worse without you in it. So please don't go. Don't die in a snowbank (please). Don't get eaten by a coyote or a moose (okay?). Don't freeze up and stop thinking (I think a lot too). Just keep going.

You asked if life gets better or if it just gets different. I'm glad you didn't have an eraser to erase that question.

Here's my answer. I think it gets better. It gets different too. But it gets better.

The reason I think this is because I'm an optimist. In the past fifteen years, I could've died a dozen times over. But I'm still here. If I didn't believe that life will keep getting better and better, then I don't think I'd still be here.

Because, what would I have to live for?

I don't exactly mean that good things will happen to me. Or great things even. I'm not saying that I'll be fabulously rich, or wildly famous, or even have the most carefree, charmed life. That's not what I'm saying. I mean, it gets better because I keep getting better.

I keep getting stronger. Wiser. More patient. More accepting. More compassionate. Life is better because even when things are so horribly hard, I tell myself that I'm thankful for whatever life brings me, whatever it's teaching me, whatever I'm given. That's why it's better.

I guess I'm philosophical about life. Someone said to me the other day, do what makes you happy. Lots of people say that. Do what makes you happy. As if the pursuit of happiness is the ultimate goal in life. Like it can excuse hurting others, hurting yourself, ignoring truths—as long as something makes you happy, then it's okay.

But if life was only about making yourself happy, then we would only care about our own desires, our own wants, our own needs. And other people, wouldn't they just become a means to an end? Your happiness? If the entire world was full of people who only cared about their own happiness, then . . . well, maybe the problem is we don't know what happiness really is or how to get there.

I think that's why I like Christmas. It reminds us that we're here to love others and to leave the world a better, kinder place than when we got here.

You don't need things to be happy. You don't really need much at all. Surprisingly, you don't even need your health to be happy.

I learned a lot this last year.

That's one of the things I learned.

I have so much to tell you, but I think after reading your letter, everything I was going to say doesn't feel as important anymore. I guess some things are more important.

Like books.

I'm joking. No. I'm not.

For me, books were my earliest friend. They always encouraged me. Never judged me. Showed me things I never knew could be. Books were bold enough to show me that I could be better. That life could be better than it was. See? There it is again. Life gets better.

If you don't think you can relate to characters, I'd recommend reading *The Hobbit*. You'll never relate to any character more than the non-human, furry-footed, fantasy creature in that beautiful book.

There are characters with integrity in that book. By the way, of course I believe you. Of course I do. I know you would never steal someone's wallet. Your moral compass is too strong.

How do I know?

I think you can tell someone's character by the words they write and the way they write them. There is something about the way you cross your t's and loop your l's that is very trustworthy. Plus, anyone who is so liberal with commas is clearly trustworthy. (I prefer periods. *Never* semi-colons. But I respect your use of commas. You are precipitously close to the edge of run-ons (and sometimes you fall over the cliff). But your commas are sprinkled in like dear friends. I like it.)

The fact is, I like you. And I think it comes down to the fact that we want to trust the people we like.

So I'm going to trust you completely. In everything. Until you give me a reason to stop.

This morning, I went ice-skating on the pond at Boden Farm. I have these old dirty brown skates from 1975 with the dullest blades. They're too big and my ankles are always sore when I'm done skating, but I can't help myself. I love the free-falling feel of gliding on ice too much.

If you're wondering, yes, everything I own is old. When you live in a house that's been in your family since 1890, you get used to it. The way I see it, anything fifty years old or younger is practically new. You should see our pots. Or our couches. Our computer is from 1998, but no one can acknowledge that it's old because compared to everything else, it's a baby.

So I drove out to the farm pond in our 1978 red and white striped Ford pickup, all bundled up in coat, mittens, scarf, and hat. The heater doesn't work, so I kept hand warmers in my pockets.

I've been skating on this farm pond for years. It's about a quarter acre. It's a cow pond in the summer, but it ices over in early December. It's so shallow, it doesn't take long. Then the mister shovels it off and drowns it with a hose until the surface is smooth as glass.

Anyone in Romeo is welcome to drive out and skate whenever they like. So I went this morning with my brother, John, and my sister, Annabel. And my cousins, Michelle and Michael (twins). And their friends from out of town, Chase and Dawn.

You asked me about my life. This is it.

Crowded.

While you have silence all around you, I don't think I've had a moment of silence in my entire life. Even at night, the old house talks to me. The stairs creak. The beams groan. The shingles on the roof play in the wind like a xylophone. The chimney sighs. The walls knock and pop. The wind sails through the plaster and moans and whistles, even on a still, windless day.

Sundays, the house is full. Every cousin, aunt, uncle, sibling, and second-half-twice-removed-relative within a hundred miles descends on the old place for Sunday dinner. It's ham with cloves and brown sugar. Mashed potatoes. Carrots. Rolls. Apple streusel and vanilla ice cream. All served on one hundred-year-old china.

Kids sit on the floor. On the stairs. Balance plates on their knees. Anyone over thirty or married gets a chair. Not necessarily at a table. There are a lot of us. But I get a chair. Of course. It's my family after all. And then you eat, and the whole place is just bouncing with noise. The house shakes with it. But in a happy way. Christmas is like that. But more.

On Christmas there are even more people here. Hundreds, it seems. With ten people to a bedroom. Sleeping on couches, in chairs, on the floor. Tucked three or four to a bed. It's bedlam. And once the first kid wakes up, I swear it sounds like an avalanche on Mount Everest when all the kids stampede down the stairs to see the tree.

I doubt this is what you meant when you asked me to describe my Christmas. No movie would ever feature my tumble down wobbly wedding cake Victorian. Or my hundred and two relatives sleeping under tables, in closets, and on every flat surface available, all for a taste of our famous Christmas streusel.

Maybe you'll understand why I had to take off for the farm pond? Even with six other people, it was loads quieter than home.

Sometimes a person can get lost in all that noise.

So I skated. The sky was this great blue expanse and it was so cold that there wasn't any moisture in the air and no clouds either. The sun sparkled down on the white snow and the ice dust on the pond. And as my skates kicked up more dust and made this *whish, whish, whish* sound, I held out my arms and felt happy. Really, truly happy.

There's tall grass around the pond, taller than the snow. It sticks out of the white mounds. There are these wheatlike stalks on the end that look like horse's hair. Little ice crystals glint on the ends of that grass. I don't know why, but I think that it's one of the most beautiful sights in the world. That ice covered grass. The icy pond.

The empty farm fields, the snow covered trees, and the great big empty sky. The smell of snow and cold air, all clean and new. My nose numb, and my fingers tingly cold.

There was a doe at the edge of the woods, stripping bark off a tree. It made me think of you.

But like I've already admitted, I think of you often.

While I was watching that deer, the toe of my dull, rickety ice skate hit a bump. I flew head, feet, then head again onto the ice. The air got knocked out of me. For a good long while, I couldn't breathe. I could hear my brother and sister shouting. I could hear my heart banging away.

But then I got my breath back, and we went home.

To get ready for Christmas.

So here it is.

On Christmas Eve Eve, December 23, every Hobday, part-Hobday, and maybe-once-maybe-not Hobday will descend on the old Victorian. For weeks before, we'll have baked, cooked, cleaned, and tried to convince the house she's bigger than she is (to no avail).

And on December 23, everyone arrives. Pretend you're there. An almost-Hobday.

The front door has a wreath. I made it five years ago at the Christmas Market. It has cardinals and holly berries in the evergreens. You'll knock and peer through the stained glass.

(By the way, I'm glad you liked the cardinals. Maybe you'll like the fawn and doe in the winter woods on this card even more.)

Outside, it'll be snowing. Our sidewalk and porch will be shoveled. We'll have candles in the windows and Christmas lights on the roofline.

I'll open the door and say, "Merry Christmas, Lee."

And then you'll step inside. It'll be noisy, but you won't mind because it's also warm (well, warm for a drafty old house). I'll take your coat, which is dusted with snow, and hang it in the closet next to everyone else's.

And then, I'll hand you a hot cocoa and a candy cane from the silver tray by the door. Which everyone gets when they arrive. Maybe you'll want a cookie too. I spent weeks baking them. Thumbprints. Gingersnaps. Molasses. Gingerbread. Maybe you'd like the iced sugar cookies. I decorated them myself. A Christmas heart, like your ornament. It's sweet, with a touch of lemon. Because I'm a firm believer sweet is only good if it comes with a bit of tart.

Then I take your arm and pull you farther inside. To the living room. You'll see our tree. It's not the perfect specimen you imagined. No, it's always the ugliest tree on the lot. The uglier, the better. Lopsided. Scraggly. Droopy. It's my family's tradition to hunt down the lame ducks of Christmas trees, sort of like the turkey pardon. We're saving the poor sap (literally) from the wood chipper.

So I'll take you to the tree and turn on the lights. I'll point out all one-hundred-plus years of handmade ornaments. My favorite is a cross-stitch nativity sampler my great-great-grandmother made in 1892. It's worn, tattered, but still beautiful.

(No. Actually. That's my second favorite. My favorite is a cheap wood heart ornament. But that one isn't on the tree. It's still hanging on my bedpost.)

Then we'll sit on the old, uncomfortable Queen Anne style couch. Right in front of the fire. Uncle Don will be playing Christmas carols on the piano. Relatives will be joining in from the kitchen, the dining room, even from upstairs if the song is shoutworthy.

At six, I'll make you a plate full of ham and mashed potatoes, but I'll warn you not to eat the carrots because they're always underdone. And then when you're full and happy, I'll take you outside, where all of us Hobdays stand in the front yard, in the snow, and light a candle, one person to the next, wishing each other Merry Christmas, Merry Christmas, Merry Christmas.

I'll light your candle, Lee.

The idea is that the warmth of the candle will fill your heart for another year.

The grandma who made the sampler started the tradition and we've never stopped.

Then when everyone is tucked in bed, or beneath a table, or wherever, you and I can lie under the Christmas tree and look up at the lights. Like they're the stars in the sky. We'll breathe in the evergreen scent.

It will be quiet under the Christmas tree. But maybe, you'll think it's the good kind of quiet. The house will still be moaning. Some of my relatives will be snoring. The snow will be whispering as it falls. The fire popping and crackling. You'll be able to hear me breathing, maybe you'll be able to hear your heart beating. But otherwise it will be quiet.

And in that quiet, I'll whisper, Merry Christmas.

And maybe you'll hear what I mean in those words.

Keep living. Keep going. Keep your integrity. Keep your goodwill. Keep being kind and good. Keep thinking and wondering. But never wonder if no one would notice if you're gone. I would.

Next year, when December arrives, please don't wonder whether or not you should write me. You should.

I'll have been waiting to hear from you. I'll still be here. Healthy. Happy. (See? Happy.) Better.

The offer remains. If you ever need a place to stay, the old ramshackle Victorian is here. No one would mind, even if you do look meaner and older than you really are. Knowing my family, they'd probably like you all the better for it.

Merry Christmas.

Yours,
    Cordelia

P.S. I included a sugar cookie for you. I baked it this morning. I bet, by the time it reaches you, it'll be crumbled, maybe even pulverized into a sugary, lemony, frosting powdered glob. But I can assure you, it was once a heart with white and blue frosting and the words *Merry and Bright.* Even if it looks frightening, it will taste good.

It's my own recipe, perfected over the years through much trial and error. It's sweet and tart. If you ever meet me, you'll appreciate it more. Although, maybe you can already appreciate it. Have a good year. I'll be thinking of you.

eight years ago

3

———————

Eight years ago

Cordelia Hobday
   1621 Tenderfoot Lane
   Romeo, NY

Dear Cordelia,

Merry Christmas. I've been waiting a long time to write that. I'll write it again. Merry Christmas.

I'm surprised to say that I stopped wondering if you'd still be alive to read my letter and started looking forward to writing you, I guess, at least three months ago. No, four. It snowed a good four inches in September and it made me think of Christmas and you.

That isn't to say I don't think of you other times. You

admitted it, so I can too. I like to think about things I can share with you. How for the past year Jackson and an ornery porcupine have become arch enemies. "That demmed porcupine. I'll gut it."

Or how, in the spring, a doe had two velvety, big-eyed fawns that followed her on shaky legs, picking their way through the undergrowth. Every time they passed, I'd hold still, barely breathing, watching their white spotted coats flicker under the dappled sun, and they never minded me, never thought I was a threat, even though the last time they passed, nearly full grown, Jackson walked outside and handed me the rifle. Jackson was pretty disappointed in me when I didn't pull the trigger, he didn't say so, but with him, you can tell. But I guess, I decided sometime between spring and late summer, that I wasn't cut out to kill something that trusted me and had, at times, made me feel not so alone. Plus, I named them, the fawns, Fili and Kili, and I guess you know, once you name something, it's nearly impossible to eat it.

By the names Fili and Kili, I guess you realize that I read *The Hobbit*. I picked it up from the library down south about two weeks after I got your letter.

I can admit there wasn't much whining or self-denial, and I did like the characters, but it wasn't Bilbo that I related to. I actually preferred the dwarves. They were gruff, sort of like Jackson and Saul, they even have the beards, but they were also hopeful. It wasn't the normal kind of hope, you know? For all they knew, everyone was dead, their home was destroyed, and they were all doomed. But they'd been hoping and believing for *years*. Normal hope is like, hey, I hope Saul remembers to pick up his prescription. Or I hope the snow plow makes it out this way soon. Or, I hope this next truck stops and gives me a ride to town.

But the dwarves had a different kind of hope. It was like they'd decided to grip it and hang on to it, *no matter what*. I guess I related to that.

For all I say that I think my family is a false memory, there's a part of me that hopes that they're real. It's like the dwarves. No matter how much my mind tries to kill it or time tries to convince me I made it all up, I still have this hope that refuses to go out. Sometimes I'd like it to, but it won't.

I had that ornament, "First Christmas" with the letters, LC. I wonder, was that LC my initials? Or is it a company, or town, or an abbreviation? I don't know. I just have fragments of a Christmas from a long time ago.

I think it was New York.

I turned sixteen this year. I think. I've counted the years, and I don't think I lost any. I count them by the people I met. Annie, with the shopping cart, in San Francisco when I was seven. Moshe who taught me to play poker in Phoenix when I was nine. Skylar in Vancouver who played guitar on the street during the days and did drugs at night when I was twelve. You, when I was fourteen, writing me a letter. And each year after, I'm counting by your letters. So I'm sixteen, almost seventeen, and I've never been back to New York City.

My first real memory I'm in Toronto and I'm hungry. That's all. Then I climb into the back of a truck and fall asleep behind some boxes. The next week, I met a twelve year old named Sherry, who was making her way to California. I stuck with her for a few months. Did I mention that I didn't talk until I was seven? I can't remember if I told you. I guess that's why I have sympathy for Jackson and Saul.

But like I said, I'm nearly seventeen, twenty-one if you go by my fake ID. And all these years I've had this hope that I refuse to admit, and because of that I've never gone back to where I think my family is. I've been afraid. You're the only person I'll admit that to. In fact, as soon as I fold this letter and put it in the card, I'll forget that I admitted it. So don't mention it, alright?

You know about fear, so maybe you'll understand. I think you will. I thought when I was seven and eight that when I was older, bigger, that I'd never have to be afraid. I guess, I didn't know enough about the world yet to realize that I wouldn't stop being afraid. I just, well, like you said, I'd just have to keep going.

So I thought about that a lot. And I thought about what you would do. I feel like I know you. I like what you said about how you can learn a lot about someone by what they write and how they write it. You're direct, with your blocky letters, and your short sentences, and your love of periods. You wouldn't hide from your fear. I imagined writing you, and I imagined what you'd say, and I decided that you'd tell me to go to New York City.

I've been afraid for years that I'd get to Manhattan and not recognize anything. I guess, I was terrified that the city would be a stranger to me, and if I didn't recognize it, and it didn't recognize me, then, would that mean, that small, resilient hope would finally die?

I never wanted to find out that the memory I always supposed was false, was in actuality, false.

What do you think? Do you agree with Jackson? Do I think too much?

But I did it. I took your imaginary advice and here I

am. Cordelia, I'm writing this long after midnight, sitting on the curb, your Christmas card on my knees, so I'm sorry if my writing is nearly illegible. I'd like to blame it on the dark, but the paper is lit by the bright streetlights and the windows still glowing in the skyscrapers overhead. So let's blame my handwriting on numb fingers and using my knees as a desk.

Maybe you saw the postage stamp, or maybe you can tell from the picture on the front of the card, but yes, I'm in New York City.

I left Stalwart Branch without any protest from Jackson or Saul. I told them over a breakfast of oatmeal and coffee. Jackson gave a sharp grunt and Saul nodded slowly, and that was all. I guess they're rubbing off on me though, because I didn't say much either.

Just, "I'm heading down with Old Freddy to sell trees in New York."

Jackson: Grunt.

Saul: Nod.

Me: "I'll be back in January."

Jackson: Nod.

Saul: Nothing.

Old Freddy has a Christmas tree farm fifty miles from Stalwart Branch. I met him at the post office last summer. He's not actually old, but he's not young either. He's called Old Freddy because when he was a baby he looked like an old man, and the name stuck.

He talks enough for fifty people, one of those that Saul claims talks and talks and never says anything at all. I don't mind it, in fact, the flow of his words is sort of like a warm blanket that you can pull around yourself. It's comforting. We drove down to the city at the end of November with a load of trees and set ourselves up on the sidewalk. Whatever you're thinking about the glamor of selling trees in Manhattan, well, don't.

Old Freddy is slick. He sprays the trees with that evergreen chemical air freshener I told you about, the one that stinks, and sticks in your nose, and burns your eyes. It doesn't smell anything like the balsam fir woods up north, it just smells like that evergreen floor cleaner they use in truck stop bathrooms. Then, at night, when we haul the trees across the bridge and park in the lot where we have our beds in the back of the pickup, Old Freddy will spray any drooping, browning tree needles with green spray paint. He has a few colors. Spruce green, grass green, apple green. He mixed them because he said the multi-hue made it more realistic.

Remember what I told you about integrity? After I saw Old Freddy spraying down the trees, I "misplaced" the cans of paint. Old Freddy bought more and I "misplaced" them again. He knows what I'm doing, and he shouts at me that an old man has to make a living, but I just tell him he can take the loss out of whatever he was going to pay me.

So every day, when he has to toss out a browning, droopy tree that he would've spray painted, he marks it down in this little black notebook as a minus in my pay column. He also marks down -10, or -15, if I forget to jack up the price when someone comes up wearing nice shoes. Old Freddy says you have to charge more if someone is wearing nice shoes. We don't have prices on the trees, you just say the price, depending on what they're wearing. I expect, by the end of December, I'm going to end up owing Old Freddy more money than he would've made even if I hadn't been here. Like I said, he's wily.

I bet, you're thinking, what about New York? Is it familiar? Do you remember it? I guess I'm avoiding that part.

No, Cordelia. I don't remember it.

Nothing is familiar. I've walked from the very southern tip, where the winds gusted in Battery Park, and the water was slate-gray and cold, all the way to the top where you dead-end at the bare-limbed, December cold trees in Inwood Hill Park.

Everyone is a stranger here. And sometimes I find myself wishing that I could find you, that in the faces of one of these strangers, I would find you. We would talk, just like we write in these letters, and as we talked, we'd walk the streets, and then my search wouldn't feel so desperate, or so lonely.

The trouble, perhaps, is that I don't know what I'm looking for. I'd like to say that I'll know it when I find it, but I don't think that's true. So I wander through the billboards and noise of Times Square, circle the ice skating rink at Rockefeller Center, pass like a ghost through the wintry frost of Central Park. For nearly a month I've haunted these streets. I pass millions of black-coated, fast-walking strangers on the street, all of them wearing the same closed-off, unwelcoming expression and I desperately search their faces and think—are you, or you, or are you—but no, I don't think they are. I guess, in this city, with all its millions of people, with everyone talking and buying and doing, I guess, Cordelia, I feel more lonely than I ever have, even when I was standing in the center of those New Brunswick woods, and no one had said a single word in at least three weeks, I feel more alone even then when I was lying in that snowbank dying, that's how New York feels. Unrecognized and lonely.

But maybe that's alright. I have one more week here, and then I'll be able to put this hope to rest. Kill it. I guess that's why I never named it and never said it out loud even to myself. It'll be easier to kill that way. When I don't find what I was looking for.

I'll go back to Stalwart Branch, to Jackson and Saul and the cabin there. I think I'll stay another year, no more than that. But you can write me there, I'll be happy to find your letter, and maybe you'll tell me to not whine like those characters in books that I don't like, but instead be grateful that I have two 900 year old surly men who may or may not care, but at least let me use their toilet, and that I had the trip of a lifetime to New York, where I sold Christmas trees with a swindler and tried to stop his scheming at least six times a day, and, did I tell you? No. I forgot. Sorry. My fingers are cramping and I'm almost out of room on the paper. I'll write smaller.

I saw the Christmas tree lighting at Rockefeller Center. It wasn't like my memory. It was better.

I wanted to tell you that the tree has 50,000 lights and a giant star, and when I saw it, it reminded me of what you wrote, how we'd lie under your tree and look up at the lights and it'd be quiet, but a good quiet. A lot of days over the last year, I thought about Christmas at your home. I read your description so many times that the paper is creased and thinned, the pencil is smudged and faded, and some of the words are just a gray blur, but since I memorized your words, I still know what it says. When I saw that tree at Rockefeller, it made me think of Christmas with you, and I felt, suddenly, like I'd been there, and we'd already spent a Christmas together. So maybe, this year, you can pretend that you're here in New York City, with me.

I know the city now. I've wandered the streets for hours, days, until I'm even walking them in my dreams. This is what Christmas would be.

You'd come by where we have our trees set up, and instead of taking you to the fullest, most perfect tree, I'd pull you to the back, where I'd saved the sorriest, ugliest, most ragged tree we have. The tree I'd saved for you so that you could give it your pardon. Then I'd tie it to the roof of your car, nice and tight, with a dozen bungee cords, so that it could make it back to Romeo in one piece. After that, I'd take you by the bakery down the block. They have chocolate yule logs in their display case that I've been eyeing for weeks. If you come, I'd buy it, because it's chocolate with crushed candy cane on top, and I think you'd like that. Although, maybe you aren't supposed to have sugar? Do you have a heart diet? I didn't think about that.

Well, this is my imagining, so in it, you're going to share a yule log with me because your heart, like you said, is healthy now, and I believe you. After the yule log, we'll get hot cocoa and walk the city. I'm almost out of room. So let me say this. I'd take you ice skating, and we'd rent new skates, so your ankles won't hurt, and you'd teach me how because I've never skated before. And we'd skate all night, right under the Rockefeller Christmas tree, and I'd make a new memory to fill up the hole that the old one left. I might not know anyone else, but I'd know you. That would be our Christmas. Cold noses, pinched toes, free-falling across the ice, and me saying, "Merry Christmas."

Please write back. Send a card with a picture of

Romeo. I've almost forgotten what it looks like. Tell me about your year. Tell me about your family and how they love you and drive you crazy. I realized, I don't know much about you. Not anything really. Which I guess is a good thing because if I knew the specifics, then maybe I wouldn't feel so free to say everything I do.

I feel myself changing. Growing. Hardening, maybe. Or freezing. When I write next year, will I be the same person? I guess I'm closing off to everyone but you.

Sometimes I worry that I won't keep getting better, like you say, but I'll get worse. But I'll try to be better, so that when I write, you'll still recognize me.

I hope your Christmas is as loud, noisy, and happy as you described it. Maybe you could light a candle for me. I'll light one for you too, there's a church around the corner, and sometimes I find myself there, looking at the flickering candles, just thinking about life.

Merry Christmas.

—Lee

P.S. I included a pop-up wood cutout of The Rink at Rockefeller Center and the Christmas tree, I bought it from a street vendor who promised you would like it. If you pull the red ribbon on the back, the two figure skaters will pirouette. I hope you like it. Please write me. Lots of people say Merry Christmas when you sell trees, but none of them say it like you do.

Dear Lee,

I'm coming. I'm coming to New York City. I'll find you.

Yours,
Cordelia

Unsent

4

———————

The thin crescent moon bathed New York in silver moonlight and outfitted the frosted skyscrapers in a fine silvered tinsel. The giant buildings glowed, illuminated by the moonlight and their own strands of Christmas lights so that the entire city was a forest of skyscrapers, naked-limbed and wrapped in glittering white and flashing red and green lights.

Thick, snow-mound white clouds had swept in from the east that morning, chasing the great black-backed and the ring-billed gulls from off the chill gray Atlantic. By noon, the clouds had lost their white glimmer and had hunkered over Manhattan, taking on the dirty gray of old snow tinged with exhaust and street dirt.

The clouds had wrapped themselves like a thick coat of gray snow around the tops of the buildings, and as

Corey tugged her wool coat tighter and then blew on her numb, gloved fingers, she wondered when the clouds would finally release the snowflakes they'd been promising for the past twelve hours. The clouds, the chill wind that whipped through the long wind-tunnel streets, and that particular scent of snowfall had been *promising* snow all day. And yet. And yet the snow still hadn't fallen.

There was an expectancy in the air, though, as if everyone in the city could sense the promise of snow. A mother clad in a down feather parka tugged her young son from the metal-fenced playground, promising hot cocoa if he'd hurry. An older woman, the top of her head barely visible outside the fur of her collar, quickly glanced at the sky, then back again at the street, waving a hand for a taxi. All day, people had swept past Corey with heads down, scarves snug over noses, hands braced around coats, buffeted by the wind.

There were snapshots of the New York at Christmas that she knew from previous years. Each moment its own Christmas card. The ice-skaters at Rockefeller twirling on smooth white ice beneath the Christmas tree. The smell of roasting, sugared almonds outside a jewel box of a toy store on Third Avenue. The piping trill of a bright red cardinal flashing against the deep green of a holly bush in Central Park.

But now, twelve hours into her search, Corey didn't want Christmas card memories or magic New York moments. She wanted Lee. Well, she wanted to find Lee.

She'd arrived at seven in the morning, with hundreds of commuters, all tumbling into Grand Central in a dizzying to-and-fro whirlwind. She was warm then, full of coffee, cinnamon-apple donuts, and expectant hope.

The expectancy had remained, just like the heavy clouds above. However, the hope was dwindling.

She'd circled around Manhattan like the cinnamon and sugar of a pinwheel cookie, spinning through each neighborhood, stopping at every Christmas tree seller in the city. She began at the bottom of the city, smiling at the cold nipping her cheeks and biting her fingers. There was the slate-gray chill of the wind rising off the water, the Statue of Liberty looking benevolently on. She circled and looped through China Town, licking the juice of dragon fruit from her fingers, and meandered to SoHo, traipsing through brick streets lined with boutiques wrapped in garland. There was the Christmas tree seller in Greenwich Village, near the bakery where she couldn't resist a hot chocolate infused with orange liqueur. That was early in the day, when she thought finding Lee wouldn't—well, it wouldn't be easy, but it wouldn't be impossible either.

By midafternoon, she'd been through the congestion of Midtown, where the cacophony of horns took on a sort-of Christmas bell ring. She'd been by Rockefeller, down Fifth Avenue, and up the Hudson to all the residential streets of the Upper West Side.

There were so many sights. So much color and flash. During the day, when she was overwhelmed, sometimes she'd spy a subway tunnel and dash down the stairs, into the soggy, humid heat, where she could close her eyes and fall into the lulling, rushing wind sound of arriving and departing trains.

It wasn't like the times she'd been before. Then she'd been with her parents and her brother and sister. She hadn't realized it then, but her parents had sheltered her. She'd felt completely safe and confident with her mittened hand in her mom's. They'd taken taxis. Gone to Rockefeller. The Met. To the Hayden Planetarium and pretended the stars were Christmas lights.

Even when she came to the renowned pediatric cardiologists in the city, she hadn't felt this overwhelmed. Then she was cocooned by the placid white walls and hushed whispers of the hospital. The city with its noise and buzz was hidden by the soundproof, tinted glass.

Maybe this is why her mom was concerned when she'd told her last night that she was going to New York in the morning. Probably it's why she insisted that Annabel come along. Likely, it's why she made Corey promise that she'd text every hour with an update that she was okay.

Her mom, after all, was a worrier. She hadn't been. Before. But when Corey turned four and they learned that she might not make it to five, her formerly unflappable mom was injected with worry, and it never fully left her bloodstream.

Annabel was twenty-one, newly married, and didn't think her almost eighteen-year-old sister needed a babysitter. So at seven fifteen she left for a day at the spa and shopping at Bloomies and told Corey to meet her back at the train platform at nine fifteen that night.

Corey had an hour before she had to flag down a taxi and run down the marble hallway, and down the station steps to meet her sister.

One hour wasn't enough time.

She knew it wasn't. She'd circled the whole city. She'd seen more tree sellers than she knew existed on this earth. She'd found tree sellers with churches around the corner. Ones with bakeries and chocolate yule logs nearby. She'd even found a tree seller that only dealt in balsam fir.

But no Lee.

Never Lee.

She grasped the Christmas card and the folded letter in her pocket. She wouldn't give up.

The wind whistled through the brick buildings of Third Avenue and Corey squinted against the cold. Her fingers were numb. Her cheeks were stinging and her nose was a little upturned block of ice. Hours ago, her feet hurt because her tall fur-lined boots were new, and blisters had popped up then burst on the backs of her ankles. But then, her feet went numb from the cold. She wasn't sorry because then she couldn't feel the scraping, burning pain from the blisters.

She'd made it to Yorkville on the Upper East Side. She'd been through earlier in the day, but realized that somehow she'd missed a ten-block section between 82nd and 92nd Street on Third Avenue.

So here she was. Her stomach was an empty cave that grumbled and whistled. She hadn't stopped for lunch, although she had bought a chocolate yule log hours ago to share with Lee when she found him. The bag had gone from light as air to feeling as if she carried three hundred pounds of rocks.

This part of the city smelled like icy river water, cold pavement, and bus diesel. Although sometimes she'd pass a restaurant, and when the door opened, she'd smell the char of grilled steak or a hint of garlic roasting. A bakery was even better because then she'd smell cinnamon with the sweet pluck of raisins, or rich chocolate melting in babka, or her favorite, melted butter with caramelized sugar.

But up ahead, she smelled something different. The forested, loamy hint of evergreen. It was subtle, then the wind picked up, and carried it closer, so that she recognized the scent. It wasn't the forest. It was the chemical replica of it. That manufactured pine aroma was so strong and nose-burning it could only have come from a bottle.

A smile tugged at her mouth, and against her will, her heart knocked around her chest, picking up speed. There was a time when every variation in her heartbeat sent her into fingernail-chewing, throat-tightening panic. It might flutter. It might speed up or slow down. It might hiccup and miss a beat. Those had frightened her the most. Some nights, she lay awake, terrified at the loud, thudding beats and the stutters of her heart.

But then, one day, she'd asked her cardiologist. And he said, your heart is normal now. It's normal for your heart to speed up when you're excited. Slow down when you lie still. It's normal sometimes for it to skip a beat. It might flutter after a cup of coffee. It's okay. It's normal.

She was *normal*.

She'd never been normal before.

So when she saw the outlines of the Christmas trees stacked along the sidewalk, she wasn't frightened that her heart had decided to tumble around her chest.

It had done the same exact thing at every Christmas tree seller she'd found today.

She quickened her pace, weaving past all the bundled-up people crowded onto the narrow confines of the sidewalk. The buildings, five and six story brick and stone apartments, some taller newer office buildings, and little businesses on the first floor, lined the street. There weren't as many Christmas lights here, not like on Fifth

Avenue or Madison, but there was still a Christmassy glow. A block back, there had been a bell ringer where Corey had dropped money and sent up a prayer that she'd find Lee before her time was up.

Ahead, a grocery store lit the sidewalk, its windowed walls spilling yellow light onto the street. The evening traffic was slower this far north of Midtown. This was mostly a residential area after all. But that meant it was the perfect place for Christmas trees.

Corey tucked her arms beneath the wool folds of her sleeves and let the bag with the yule log bang against her thigh. Now that she was closer, she saw that the seller took up nearly half a block. There were all different types of trees. Not that she knew them all by sight, but she at least recognized the tight blue needles of a blue spruce and the hunter green of a balsam fir. There had to be at least fifty trees. All sizes, all shapes, all types.

There was a family of three, with the little girl begging for a tree at least seven feet tall. There was a woman looking at a miniature potted evergreen with soft frondlike branches. A couple debated whether or not a Norwegian pine was the perfect first Christmas tree as newlyweds or not.

Corey searched the sidewalk, trying to find the seller. Lee. Or Old Freddy. Either one.

This was maybe the last Christmas tree seller in Manhattan. She couldn't guarantee that she'd been to them all, but it felt like it. Her eyes stung. They felt like they did after a long cry, but she wasn't crying. It was the overpowering scent of evergreen. Corey bent close and looked at the needles of the nearby blue spruce. She couldn't tell if they were painted, so she took off her glove and rubbed her cold-numb fingers over the slippery, prickly needles.

Her heart, never before so trigger-happy, kicked around when a bit of green paint rubbed off between her pointer finger and her thumb.

She'd found him.

This had to be him.

Her cheeks heated. Her whole body, which had been cold for hours, suddenly was as warm as if she was sitting in her family's living room in front of the fire, a knitted blanket on her lap, drinking her mom's hot cider.

Corey wasn't exactly sure why she was so compelled to come to New York. She didn't exactly know why it was imperative for her to find Lee. But something in his letter grabbed her last night and wouldn't let go. As soon as she'd found the letter in the mailbox she'd torn it open and unfolded the sheets of paper. She'd read it under the starlight, her breath fogging in the cold air. And with each line and each beat of her heart she'd heard him.

I need you. That's what he'd said. It wasn't written in the letter. In fact, he never said it at all. But she could read it there. It was like the snowflakes that fell and then melted in the warmth of her hand. There, then gone. That's how she knew. She'd seen the snowflakes. She'd felt his words. He needed her.

So she would go to him. Find him.

She didn't know exactly what she'd do when she found him. She didn't know what she'd say. She hadn't gotten that far. She only knew he needed her, and she had to find him.

She knew it deep inside. Like a homing pigeon always knew how to fly home. Or an apple seed knew how to grow into a tree. Or how her grandma knew exactly how much butter her sugar cookies required, just by touch. It was exactly like that. Corey knew that Lee needed her and she had to go to him.

It was only now, when she was sure that she was about to meet him that she wondered what he'd think of her.

Seventeen, almost eighteen. Too small, too skinny, stunted growth—most people said it was because her heart had required all her body's concentration and there wasn't enough left for her to grow as tall as her sister or her mom. She had auburn hair, or red if you weren't romantic. Corey wasn't very romantic, so she usually called it red. But today, she'd call it auburn. Freckles, as many freckles as Christmas lights strung on a tree. Green eyes and long eyelashes, which she thought were her best feature. A small, thinnish nose. Wide lips that usually were smiling. Today, she was bulky and bundled in a navy wool coat, a thick wool sweater, long johns, jeans, wool socks and her fur-lined boots. And she was still pink-cheeked, red-nosed, and freezing cold. Her hair was tangled and matted under her hat and her skin was dry from the wind.

Corey shrugged. She didn't expect any of that would matter. Lee didn't care what she looked like. In fact, he'd said he liked that they hadn't met and didn't know each other in real life because then they were able to tell each other the things they'd never share otherwise.

But this was important. Important enough to break that understanding.

Corey slipped her glove back on and then looked down the sidewalk, glowing from the string of Christmas lights threaded over a few trees and the silver glow of the moon.

It was then that she saw him.

He was loading a Christmas tree onto the roof of a red Volvo. He wasn't in a coat or a hat. Just ripped jeans, a faded red flannel shirt, and scuffed leather boots. It was as if he was standing in seventy-degree weather, completely impervious to the cold. He lifted the large fir tree as if it weighed as much as a sack of flour and then tied it down.

Corey stood motionless, knocked senseless by the sight of him. She wasn't certain, but for a moment there, she thought she forgot to breathe. It was as if a heavenly choir, a trumpeting crowd of angels, broke free through the thick gray clouds and began to sing. The light from the grocery store fell over his darkened form, and goose bumps ran over her as she absorbed the full impact of him.

He was tall. She was right. The top of her head would barely reach his wide shoulders.

He was lean and rangy, his muscles long, so that he moved like the animals of the forest he wrote her about. The fox gliding between the trees, or no, maybe the wild coyotes darting and playing in the night. There was something so other about him. So separate and apart.

He didn't have the air that every other person she'd run across in her life had. That civilized air you get from growing up in a town, among people you know, going to school, eating three meals every day, and having a warm bed every night. As much as she disliked them, there was something civilizing about four walls. He didn't have that air. In fact, if civilization was a meal, this boy had never eaten a morsel in his whole life.

He was seventeen (well, almost), just like her. Although he was right. He did look older. But not meaner.

Something about the messy length of his black hair and the deep-set dark brown of his eyes was disarming. He was as dark as she was red, and she expected he was as hard to crack in person as she was as easy to read.

But it was him. It was Lee.

She'd found him.

She pulled in three rapid breaths, fog puffing out in front of her. Her heart was galloping, urging her forward. So she took a step toward him. The cold wind tugged at her and blew her knitted navy scarf free to flap behind her. She ignored it.

This was what destiny felt like. She was sure of it.

He'd finished tying the tree down. He bent over and ruffled the little boy's hair and then gave the mom and dad a friendly wave, a half-smile curving his mouth.

Corey felt her own lips twitching and responding to that smile.

He was beautiful.

He didn't tell her he was beautiful.

But boys, or men she supposed, didn't think like that. Besides, it didn't matter. They were meant to be confidants, friends who were there for each other in bad, worse, good, and better. Every Christmas, ever after. So what he looked like didn't matter.

But even knowing that, it was hard not to feel her limbs tingling, her cheeks flushing, and her breath coming short.

And then, as Corey took another step forward, something alerted him that she'd been watching. He stepped onto the curb, pulled his leather work gloves from his pocket, and then paused and looked up. Directly at her.

At that moment, the clouds finally kept their promise. It began to snow.

First one flake, then another. And from one breath to the next, the busy, pine-scented, New York street was transformed into a snow globe. Delicate white snowflakes fell around them, glittering in the yellow streetlight. They landed, whisper soft on the needles of the Christmas trees. They even landed in Lee's black hair, on his shoulders, and on Corey's eyelashes. She blinked them away.

When she opened her eyes Lee was walking toward her. His head was tilted slightly to the side, and there was a wrinkle on his forehead as if she were a puzzle he was trying to work out. Maybe he felt it too. After years of writing, they recognized each other without having ever met.

Corey couldn't wait any longer. She hurried forward, a quick spring in her step, nearly shouting with the bubbling laughter rising up in her throat.

She'd found him.

They still had an hour. They'd eat the chocolate yule log she'd bought. They'd drink hot cocoa. Maybe Old Freddy would let him off for an hour to ice-skate. They'd talk, and she'd hug him and tell him, in words instead of letters on the page, that even if he didn't find his family, he had her. And maybe, if he didn't mind, that could be enough.

She knew it was only one letter a year, but maybe, if he wanted, they could write more.

And then he was standing in front of her. She tilted her head up and raised her chin so that she could smile at him. He was warm. She could feel the warmth coming off him. And he smelled like pine and fir, with an overlay of freshly sawed wood and pine sap.

He looked down at her boots, surely calculating how much to charge her for a tree, and she almost laughed.

When he looked back up, Corey nearly took one last step forward to throw her arms around him.

"Looking for a Christmas tree?"

His voice was rough, deep, with an intonation that rolled up and down, like a rockslide in winter. She shivered as it collided with her and rolled through her.

The sound of it grabbed her insides and twisted them around and around until she was tied up in him.

So this is what love felt like.

She'd always wondered.

She smiled at him. It was an unguarded smile. The kind you give someone you've known and loved for years. Someone who knows all your secrets and still cares for you—no, loves you—even though. She gave him a smile that warmed her from the inside out and took another step forward.

He frowned, shook his head and took a step back. A bit like a forest animal, uncertain and gun-shy.

But he didn't need to be scared of her. She was Cordelia. And he was Lee.

"No," she said, "not a tree. I got here this morning, on the train. I came as soon as I could. I've been slogging through the freezing, wretched cold all day just to find—" she was rambling she knew, but she couldn't help it, she was so glad, so unbelievably glad that she'd found him. "Find y—"

She was about to say "you."

But then the word caught in her throat and was cut off like a tree chopped at its base. Because the flannel that he was wearing had a name tag. It was a rectangular patch with a name stitched in glossy red embroidery.

It said *Chris*.

She stared at the name as the snow swirled around them.

Chris.

It wasn't love. It wasn't anything. She hadn't found Lee. He needed her and she hadn't found him.

And that, more than anything, broke her heart.

5

NEW YORK, NY
    Lee

The snow had finally arrived. At first, it fell in delicate clusters, but then, as if emboldened by the first few that dared to fall, the sky let loose a flurry of lush, fat, spinning flakes.

Lee barely noticed them collecting on the boughs of the blue spruce and the Fraser fir lining the sidewalk next to him. It wasn't as if the snow would stick. Mostly, it would melt as soon as it hit the steam-vented sidewalks or the slick streets, warmed by taxis and buses.

Old Freddy would be happy, though. There was something about snow that made people desperate for Christmas trees. And with only three days left until Christmas, Old Freddy himself was desperate to unload the last remaining stock. The leftovers he'd chip up and sell as mulch, which didn't get him nearly as much dollar for dollar. Lee already knew that any tree left standing was coming out of his final pay.

Not that he was here to make money. Not really. No, he was here for one reason only. To see if New York was familiar. Or to see if he could find his family. But after nearly a month of wandering the winter-cold streets and watching, hawk-eyed, both New Yorkers and tourists shoulder past the tree stand, Lee was certain of one thing —he'd never been to New York before. It had all been a dream. Some false memory planted in his subconscious. He'd been right when he admitted his fear to Cordelia. Whoever those people in his memory were, they weren't his family. There was no Rockefeller, no Christmas tree with a popcorn garland and carols played on an old piano, no brother, mom, or dad.

It was entirely likely that the "First Christmas" ornament he'd held onto for years wasn't even his. Maybe, as a four-year-old, he'd stolen it and made up a story that after the hundredth telling became truth.

He was prosaic, though. Pragmatic. He'd never found any reason to be upset about a fact of life. The fact was, New York wasn't his home. Another fact: he didn't have a family. But he did have a job, a cabin to go back to in three days, and maybe, a Christmas card waiting for him when he got back.

He didn't want to admit it because he'd never needed anyone before, but he needed Cordelia's letter like someone dying of hypothermia needed warmth. He'd never opened up to anyone before, not in his whole life. So to do that three years in row? She was the closest thing to a friend he had. To be honest, she was more than that.

She was the mooring that kept him steady throughout the year. She was the guide when he questioned what he should do or who he should become. She was—now that he was flailing and uncertain with the realization that the New York he saw in his memory was a figment of his imagination—she was the only person who he could claim as his and who could also claim him.

Lee smiled over at the little boy, jumping up and down next to the station wagon as he tied the Christmas tree to the family's car roof. The cold stung his cheeks, but he didn't mind. He liked the cold. He especially liked how the sharp, snow-tinted air mixed with the diesel and fake pine smell to keep him awake and energized. If you were cold—but not too cold—then you wouldn't fall asleep. Drinking lots of coffee also helped. During his eighteen-hour days peddling Old Freddy's trees he drank at least eight cups of coffee.

The cheap kind. The little eight ounce Styrofoam dollar cups filled with milk and sugar from the tiny deli at the end of the block. He liked burning his tongue on the hot, bitter liquid. He liked how the warmth spread down into his chest and then through all his limbs, even to his toes.

The parents he'd sold the tree to said thank you. The little boy jumped up and down again, and Lee ruffled his hair. It was hard not to get caught up in how much kids loved Christmas. And listen to him. Some people would think *he* was still a kid, but Lee knew he hadn't been a kid for at least twelve years.

He smiled at that. Like he said, there wasn't any use being upset about a fact. The wind whipped down the narrow tunnel of the sidewalk, using the buildings as a slide to whirl down. Snowflakes kicked around him, landing on his shoulders and melting on his cheeks. One landed on his lips, and he licked off the cold iciness just as it melted.

It was getting late. The sky was dark except for that tiny sliver of moon. The rush of traffic had slowed now that it was after seven, and the headlights that speared the darkness were muted by the snowfall. Maybe he'd get another coffee soon or a quick hot sandwich. Although, if he were right, the snow would bring in a rush of people wanting firs, pines, and spruces.

He shrugged his shoulders, rolled them, and stretched. In a few hours, Old Freddy and he would pack up the truck. Then maybe if it was still snowing, he'd walk the city.

Not looking for his family or the Christmas in his memories, but instead looking for . . .

Cordelia?

All day long, he'd had a feeling. Like she was here. Like if he looked hard enough or thought about her long enough, she'd appear right in front of him.

It was an itch along the back of his neck as if he could sense her standing behind him, watching him work. Sometimes, he felt a weight on his forearm, as if she was resting her hand—right there—where he'd rolled up his sleeves.

It wasn't going to happen. He knew this. He'd only written her two days ago. She might not even have received his letter yet. And if she had, why would she come to New York? And if she did. Well. What did she look like?

He didn't know.

Sometimes he pictured her like the grandmother he'd always wanted. Tall and plump enough for a good hug, with short white hair and softly wrinkled skin that folded like an old creased leather bag. She'd have a thousand laugh lines and sharp green eyes full of humor and warmth. He imagined she'd smell like sugar cookies and lemon zest, and when he went to her rickety old house, she'd welcome him inside and give him a hard, lemon-scented hug.

But he didn't know. Maybe she wasn't that old.

Eighty was likely. After all, she was friends with octogenarians, played cards at the retirement center, and had already had three heart surgeries. But she wrote like she was younger. Her strong, blocky letters weren't the spidery thin lines of a grandma's scrawl. So maybe she was forty or fifty, and she'd been unlucky enough to have heart problems earlier than seventy or eighty.

Either way. She was old.

Anyone named Cordelia was old.

When he wrote her he didn't think about her age. She was a person outside of time, but looking for her? She was old.

So that left him discreetly studying the face of every woman aged forty to ninety who walked by, wondering ... is that her? Could that be her?

It was the same thing he'd done when looking for his family.

He needed to stop.

This was the trouble with needing someone. You forgot how to rely on yourself because you wanted to rely on them. Or at least, share your troubles with them.

So. He'd stop.

He shook his head. Tomorrow, he'd stop. Tonight, he'd keep looking for Cordelia.

He pulled his leather gloves free from his pocket, ready to reorganize the line of trees when he saw her.

It was a girl.

The snow really picked up then, and if you hadn't noticed it snowing before, you'd notice it now.

The girl stood on the sidewalk, nearly a bus-length away, half-hidden by a balsam fir. Lee stopped walking, his muscles going rigid at the painful tingle that worked over his skin. The back of his neck prickled, and his ears burned as if they'd been ice cold and then splashed with steamy hot water. There was a sort of live electric socket going off inside him, and for the life of him, he couldn't figure out why.

Maybe it was because the girl was alone.

He hated it when he saw little kids alone.

She was tiny. Maybe she topped five feet, but probably not. It was hard to tell. She was bundled in layers and layers of winter gear. A fuzzy blue hat, a thick red scarf knitted with bulky yarn, a navy wool coat, and winter boots with fuzzy gray fur. From far off, he couldn't see her very well, but he had the vague impression that her hair was brown, her eyes were brown, her cheeks were very, very pink, and her nose was very, very red.

He took a quick glance around the sidewalk, trying to find her parents. No one was paying her any attention. All the New Yorkers were hurrying by, carrying grocery bags, briefcases, or pushing strollers. She was alone.

His chest pinched, and he had to remind himself that she wasn't him. She didn't seem scared or lost.

He shoved his leather gloves back in his pocket and started toward her.

But as he strode closer, he realized he'd been mistaken. She wasn't a child. She was a teenager. At least fifteen. Maybe even seventeen. Young, but not so young that she couldn't be alone.

Then she smiled at him and Lee nearly tripped over his own feet. Her smile punched him in the gut, knocked him in the head, and left him confused, irritated, and a little resentful. How could she smile at him like that? She was smiling at him as if she *loved* him. He couldn't mistake it, even though he'd never received a look like that before. Her face was glowing and it was glowing for him.

Lee clenched his hand, digging his cold fingers into the meaty part of his palm, and reminded himself that girls this sweet, this clean, this pretty—she *was* pretty— didn't smile at boys like him. Not like this.

She didn't know what she was doing.

And she especially didn't know what she was doing to him.

Now that he was close, he saw that her hair wasn't brown. It was red. In the dark, the Christmas lights picked up strands of auburn and gold. It was too dark to tell, but he thought her eyes were hazel with a hint of green. She smelled good. Like chocolate and orange.

She was still smiling at him. He didn't know why, but it made him think of Cordelia. Maybe, with her grandma smile, she'd look at him a bit like this too. Understanding and warmth, happiness and acceptance.

There was a hollow hunger inside him, an empty space, and there was something there that told him she could fill it.

He gave her a tight smile. Looked down at her boots to gather himself, then up at her again.

"Looking for a Christmas tree?"

At his question, her eyes widened and then a red

flush spread over her pale skin so that she looked almost like a bright red holly berry covered in snow. And then that smile she'd had before? It'd been nothing. Because after his question, she smiled again. And this smile was like waking up after nearly dying of cold, freezing in a snowbank, and finding her with a blanket and a fire, her arms wrapped around him in a tight hug.

Holy ever-loving goodness.

Who was she?

All the blood rushed from Lee's head and left him dizzy and stunned.

"No, not a tree." Her voice was quiet and rough-scraped like she had a cold or had shouted and lost her voice. He stared, enthralled by the sound. "I got here this morning, on the train. I came as soon as I could. I've been slogging through the freezing, wretched cold all day just to find . . ."

She took a step forward. Lee frowned and took a step back. If she came any closer he'd want to touch her to see if she was really real.

"Find . . ." She paused. "Y—" Cut off.

A line formed between her brows as she stared at his chest. He blinked, wondering what she was talking about, and what she'd been about to say.

A tree?

Had she been looking all day for a tree?

"A tree?"

He watched her politely, keeping his expression neutral, although he was a little worried with how all the color had drained from her face.

"Chris!"

Lee looked down the sidewalk. Old Freddy waved his

arm sharply and gestured for him impatiently. Lee looked to the girl. "Sorry. I'll be right back."

He waited until she nodded and then hurried to Old Freddy.

"Load their white pine, alright Chris? Do a good job."

Lee grunted, then while the family watched, he spun twine around the tree, wrapping it tight, and loaded it in the back of their SUV. While he worked, he kept glancing back at the girl to make sure she was still there. He didn't know why he was nervous that she'd leave. Potential customers and browsers left all the time. She didn't move from where he'd left her though. She just stared at the gray concrete sidewalk, shaking her head and gesturing like she was arguing with herself.

Once the pine was loaded and the family had driven off, Old Freddy slapped Lee on the back. "Good job, Chris."

Lee sighed. "Do you have to call me Chris?"

"It's funny. Just like you call me Nick, eh? Customers like it. Chris Kringle and Old Nick. Christmas Tree Purveyors. You got one on the line?" Old Freddy glanced over at the girl and squinted at her shoes, just like Lee knew he would. "Charge her fifty percent more. Those are expensive boots."

Lee didn't answer, just hurried down the sidewalk, back through the passing evening crowd and the flurrying snowflakes, to the girl. He was out of breath, even though he'd barely taken twenty steps to reach her. He blinked against the cold and the snow.

"You're still here."

She looked up at him, and he felt heat prickle his cheeks at the inaneness of his statement.

She frowned and then nodded.

"Have you been looking all day for a tree?" He put his hands in his pockets, unsure for the first time in his life what to do with them. He wanted to reach out and take her hands, so he buried them in his pockets instead, and with his right hand, he gripped the warm, smooth metal of his lucky penny.

"Sort of." Then she nodded, a yes, then a no. "I mean ..." She flinched, then shrugged. "I don't really know."

Lee raised his eyebrows. Maybe the girl whose smile had punched him in the gut wasn't all there in the head. Not that he would judge her for it.

"Well, we have lots of trees. Fraser fir. White pine. Balsam fir. Blue spruce."

"Do you have any ugly ones?"

Lee gave a surprised laugh. It sort of burst from him, and then he looked at the girl more closely.

"What do you mean?"

That's exactly the sort of thing Cordelia would ask.

"Well. I've been to exactly thirty-seven Christmas tree sellers today. And not a single one of them had a small, stunted, ugly, bound for the wood-chipper Christmas tree. How wrong is that?"

When she got to her last words, Lee was grinning. His cheeks tingled from the cold and the width of his smile. He'd been tired before, the long day wearing him down, even with all the caffeine. He'd been cold and hungry too. And, he'd admit it, lonely. He'd wanted, no needed, a friend. Cordelia, he'd thought.

But here was this ridiculous, tiny girl, with her preposterous statements and her wide doe-like eyes that just looked right into him. In this forest of Christmas trees, all lined up on the busy sidewalk, their branches shielding them from traffic, Lee felt as if she'd reached right out, like a deer spotting him from the forest, and let him know he wasn't alone.

"I can find you an ugly tree."

She tilted her head, questioning. "Can you?"

He gave a firm nod, his heart kicking him in the rib cage.

Then he took her up and down the sidewalk, pointing out the white pine Old Freddy had spray-painted from brown to hunter green that morning, the spindly Fraser fir with half its needles already shed, the blue spruce so smothered in pine scent that his eyes burned every time he passed. She shook her head at each one. None of them were ugly enough.

Then she stopped in front of a knee-high, drunkenly tilted, crackly, brown-needled, spiky pine that had been slotted for the trash. Earlier today, Old Freddy had demanded Lee throw it out. It was beyond the saving graces of spray paint and fake evergreen-scented spray.

"What's that?" The girl pointed at the potted plant.

"You don't want that one."

She turned and frowned at him. "Who says?"

Lee shook his head. It was one thing to sell her an ugly tree, it was another to sell her something that was beyond help and destined for the dump.

"I can't sell it to you."

"Why not?"

"Because it's not for sale. It's . . . not up to standard."

The girl put her hands on her hips and stared at him as if she were looking down at him, although that would've been impossible.

"It's up to my standard. I want it."

"It's practically dead. Look. The needles are brown. The trunk is weak. It probably has root rot. It's past ugly.

It's unsaveable. The pot is cheap, ugly plastic. Nobody in their right mind would want this tree. Look over there." He pointed to a gnarled blue spruce with a crooked top. "There's a perfectly ugly tree."

But her mouth was a straight, stubborn line. "I like this ugly tree. In fact, the more you tell me I shouldn't have it, the more I want it."

"Oh. You're one of those."

She made a huffing noise, half-laugh, half-affronted snort. "One of what's?"

"Do-gooders. You'll save this ugly, half-dead, worthless tree, and then you'll expect it to owe you homage for the rest of your life."

She laughed and the sound traveled up his spine and sent a buzz riding over his skin.

"What's your name?" she asked, looking at the name embroidered on his shirt.

He sighed. Who cares if he was Chris or if he was Lee? He'd never see this girl again. He pointed a finger at the name on his chest. Tapped the letters.

"Chris like Christmas?"

"Right."

It didn't feel right telling her that, but now it was too late. She was already talking.

"Well, Chris like Christmas. I like you. And because I like you and I'm only in this city for another hour, I'll make you a deal. You are going to sell me that ugly, stinky, unfortunate tree. What type of tree is it again?"

She lifted an eyebrow and waited.

He resisted the urge to smile. "A dwarf Alberta."

"Ah. Exactly like I thought."

He tried not to laugh. She'd had no idea what kind of tree it was.

"You are going to sell me this ugly dwarf Alberta, and because I'm so thrilled, I'll share my chocolate yule log with you. I don't have forks, so we'll eat it with our hands."

She pulled the white paper sack from off her arm and opened it, showing him a white bakery box tied with red ribbon.

"I've been lugging it around for hours, and the thing's so heavy I think my arm's about to fall off."

"A chocolate yule log?" His throat was tight when he looked from the package back to the girl.

She smiled again and shrugged. "If you want?"

He nodded. The back of his eyes were burning. "Sure."

"Good. Because I should really go in"—she pulled back her coat sleeve and looked at her watch—"twenty minutes. And I'm not lugging it around anymore. Besides, it'd make you happy to eat it, wouldn't it? You look like you could use cheering up."

Was it that obvious? Lee tried on a smile and then shook his head.

"Alright. You can have the ugly tree."

She smiled. "I'll give you twenty-five dollars."

"Five." He hated charging even that much, but Old Freddy would be on him like sap on pine if he didn't charge something.

"Twenty-five and not a penny less."

"You're haggling the wrong way." He frowned at her as she unwound the red ribbon and opened the bakery box. "Seven dollars then."

"Twenty-five." She held the box up and waved the yule log under his nose. The scent of chocolate wafted between them. There weren't any crushed candy canes, but it was covered in curled chocolate shavings and crushed chocolate sandwich cookies so that the frosting beneath looked like bark. "I'll pay twenty-five and not a cent less. It's worth at least that much, even if no one else can see it. In fact, I'd say it's the most interesting tree here. Wouldn't you?"

He couldn't disagree. In fact, the rich chocolate smell was making him dizzy. She held out the box to him.

"Here. Just swipe your finger through it. I'll stay on my side. You stay on yours."

She was so odd. What kind of person haggled up on a price and then shared a cake with a stranger? Eating it with her fingers?

She smiled at him as if she knew exactly what he was thinking. Then she drew her finger through the yule log and popped the chocolate glob into her mouth.

"Good." She chewed quickly, her eyes bright, and then went for another swipe and bite. "Come on. Eat."

He looked quickly at Old Freddy. He was down the sidewalk, busy with an older couple and a Fraser fir.

There was a strange buzzing inside of Lee and an odd thumping in his chest. Some mornings, when he woke up and the cabin was silent, and so were the woods, he'd feel this same thing, as if something were about to happen, something incredible. Nothing ever did. But this time, he thought, maybe, something would.

He dragged his finger through the cake. The frosting was cold and slippery, and the cake crumbled beneath the pressure of his pointer finger. Bits of curled chocolate and cookie stuck to the frosting on his finger. He put it in his mouth.

It was sweet. Rich. The bittersweet chocolate was sugary and addictive. He took another bite and then another until the girl was laughing and he was grinning as they huddled over the bakery box devouring the chocolate yule log.

Their fingers knocked together as they met in the middle. The girl giggled, a funny, husky sound that he thought might be rare for her, but he wasn't sure. He didn't know her. All the same, he laughed when she swiped a chocolate cookie bit off his finger and popped it in her mouth, then stole the last of the cake from his side of the box.

He was happy. Sugar-full and warm. He felt so happy.

In fact, standing in the silver light of the moon and the twinkling of the Christmas lights, holding a cold, empty bakery box, Lee figured this was the best Christmas he'd ever had.

No one but Cordelia had ever given him a gift. Not that he could remember. This chocolate yule log was the only Christmas gift he'd ever gotten besides his lucky penny and that crumbled sugar cookie.

"What's your name?" He stared at the bottom of the box, where the gold foil peeked out from under the smeared frosting and shimmered in the light.

"Corey." She sighed. It was a happy sound. "I'm so full. That was good. Wasn't it good?"

He looked at her. Nodded. They were closer than he'd thought. Her cheeks were pink, her lips wet from licking them, and her eyes were a bright, laughing hazel.

Corey. With her funny hunt for an ugly tree and her chocolate yule log. Maybe all his thinking about Cordelia had conjured this girl and brought her to him. Just a bit of Christmas magic. Someone who made him feel not so alone. Wasn't that strange, since in a few minutes she'd close up the box, throw it away, take the ugly tree, and walk out of his life.

Maybe in a few decades he'd think she was a false memory too.

But not now. Right now this was real.

He wished he was better with words. He could write. Back when he was younger, he'd spent a summer learning to read and write from Clark Unger, a former elementary teacher, homeless now, but Lee had paid him five dollars a day, and Clark had instilled in him enough discipline to write and write and read and read so that, in Clark's words, nobody nowhere could ever take advantage of him. Lee looked at it a different way. He learned to read and write so he wouldn't fail his future self. But reading and writing were different from talking. And he'd gotten out of practice from spending a whole year in silence.

So all the words he wanted to say got jumbled up and tangled in his chest and he wasn't quick enough to unknot them.

"Well. I'd better go. Thank you for the ugly tree. And for sharing my chocolate yule log. And for . . . well, I don't know. I guess . . ." She looked into his eyes again and smiled more shyly than she'd smiled before. "Merry Christmas."

He nodded. There was a hard lump in his throat.

This girl was the first person to tell him Merry Christmas and to mean it. She really meant it.

She held out her hand for him to take. He looked down then slid his hand into hers. Her fingers were cold and small, sticky from the cake. She squeezed his hand. And even though her fingers were cold a warmth spread up his arm and into his chest.

He shook his head. She was so strange. What sort of girl shook hands after sharing a cake? He didn't know. What he did know though was that he lived in the middle of nowhere with two hermit brothers. Who was he to say what was strange and what wasn't.

Besides, he liked her. That's all there was to it. He'd liked her immediately and the liking had only gotten stronger. But that wasn't something that was easy to say.

"Thank you. Thanks for the yule log. Thanks for . . ." He cleared his throat. "Merry Christmas."

She let go of his hand, then pressed twenty-five dollars into his palm. Two crumpled bills pulled from her coat pocket. She grabbed the dwarf Alberta by the lip of the plastic pot and held it against her chest. The dwarf tree was small but looked larger in her arms.

He felt a smile tug at the edge of his lips. He wished he could get to know her better.

"I'm going to try to have a really, really wonderful Christmas. I hope you do too." She took a step backward, moving away from him.

She'd left the empty bakery box with him. He held it in front of him as she took another step back. The people on the sidewalk moved around her. The breeze ruffled her hair and he felt both wonderfully happy and horribly bereft at the same time.

Being human was complicated. That was all there was to it.

It seemed she expected him to say something. To give some acknowledgment that he'd have a happy Christmas.

So he nodded and lifted his hand in goodbye.

"I will," he promised. Then as she smiled and turned to go, he called after her, "Merry Christmas."

He stayed there, holding the empty bakery box, until she disappeared in the crowd of faceless New Yorkers.

The snow had stopped falling. It was officially cold.

At that, Lee carefully pulled the chocolate-coated gold foil from the bottom of the box, folded it into a small square, and put it in his pocket.

6

<hr>

Lee Weston
   12933 E. Beaver Lake Road
   Stalwart Branch, NB
   Canada

Dear Lee,

I'm writing you from the utility sink in the basement laundry room. I'm sitting, knees tucked into my chest, a notebook perched on my legs, on a nest of damp socks and wrung-out sweaters that were hand-washed earlier today but not yet laid out to dry.

When I get up, there will be a wet patch on the seat of my pants, and all the little cousins will laugh and tease me. But it's worth it. The house, as you probably know, is overrun with Hobdays. All nine-hundred-and-sixty-seven of us. This is only a *slight* exaggeration.

Right now, the Croton-on-Hudson Hobday branch are having a snowball fight in the front yard. I can hear their screams and shrieks. The Connecticut Hobdays are in the kitchen. It's their turn to cook the Christmas Eve Eve dinner. It's less a structured military campaign and more a wagon train that's fallen apart. The fire alarm has gone off *nine* times, the fire department came and left with a tray of pies, and the house smells like burnt sweet potatoes, burnt goose, and burnt carrots.

We Hobdays rotate years. Each branch of the family cooks every fourteen years. The last time the Connecticut Hobdays cooked, our oven broke, the kitchen sink pipes burst, and we all went out to Boden's Diner for fried fish instead of soppy, burnt, greasy roasted duck confit.

That isn't all. Annabel and John (my brother and sister) are leading the little kids in choir practice so that on Christmas Day they can all sing, "The Twelve Days of Christmas." It's a lost cause. Only three of the fifteen kids can even count to twelve yet. Through the floorboards I can hear John banging on the piano to the shouts of "the tenth day of fifth day of two!"

I've wanted to write you since yesterday, but as you can probably tell I haven't had a second to myself. So here I am.

I dodged a snowball out front, tiptoed past the gingerbread house making in the dining room, slunk by the carolers in the living room and slipped down to the basement. It's spooky down here. Cold, drafty. The walls are stone and the floor is hard-packed dirt. Our washer and dryer are in the back corner next to a shelf full of cleaning supplies.

This corner smells like damp earth, wet stone, and laundry detergent. The shouting, the music and the beeping of the fire alarm are all hushed and muted by the vibrating whir of the dryer. It's kicking out a bit of heat, keeping me warm.

I've left the lights off just in case someone decides to look for me down here. My paper is illuminated by the tiny slit of light shining through the glass-block basement window.

I'm sorry if this is hard to read or if my lines slant down, like letters sliding down a hill. I guess this is the year of illegible letter writing.

But anyway. Here I am. Hidden away, tucked in a sink, writing to you. The sink, if you didn't know, is where the light from the window falls.

I looked for you.

I know that's an abrupt change of topic. But I looked for you.

I received your Christmas card two days ago. I held the red envelope to my chest, then ripped it open. I read your words so quickly I could barely take them in. Then I read your letter again more slowly.

I know you didn't ask. You didn't even hint this. But I felt, well, I felt as if I had to go to New York to find you. As if you needed me.

Maybe you didn't. Maybe you'll laugh when you read this. Or maybe you'll be upset because we have an understanding that we can write each other like this exactly because we don't know each other.

I guess, it doesn't matter. I didn't find you.

But I wanted you to know that I came to New York City, and I spent a day searching the streets for a black-haired, dark-eyed boy selling Christmas trees. One who looked both older and meaner than he really was. I didn't find you.

I'm sorry. When the train pulled out of New York, I felt . . . it's hard to describe. I felt unfinished. As if I'd forgotten something. Or left something behind. You, I guess.

So I'm sorry I didn't find you. And if you're upset that I looked, I'm sorry I looked, and I'm sorry I didn't find you.

No. I'm not sorry I looked.

You're my friend. We decided that years ago. I won't be sorry looking for a friend when I think he needs me.

Do you think that you can change the past? Or reinterpret it. Reimagine it.

Here's what I'm thinking.

Were you in New York on December 22?

That's the day I came.

Do you remember how cold it was? How all day long the smell of snow was thick. How the clouds hung low? Do you remember the cold wind and the crescent moon?

I don't know where you were in the city, but I bet you felt the wind, and I bet you remember the clouds and the moon. Now, think of that time, just after dusk. The sky had gone from purple gray to silver and all the Christmas lights were glowing. And then, it started to snow.

Do you remember?

I thought that New York looked like a snow globe. The snowflakes were so fat and white and they fell like feathers. Do you remember?

I was in the city. You were in the city. We stood under the same crescent moon, watching the snow fall.

That's how close we were.

You weren't alone. New York wasn't faceless that day. I was there.

The city might not have been familiar. Your family

might not be there. Sure, that's lonely. That's hard. But you weren't entirely alone. I was there.

That's all. That's all I wanted to tell you.

I don't have any words of comfort or advice. Maybe it was all a false memory. Maybe not. You're right, sometimes we can wish things into being that never really existed. But I don't think you should give up hope entirely. Someday, you might find your family. Or someday you might make a family. I wouldn't give up hope.

By the way, I'm glad you're staying in Stalwart Branch next year. I like the idea of you having a home. I never knew you when you didn't, but I don't like the thought of you all alone. The hermit brothers, as you call them, seem . . . good. I mean, they seem like good people. They saved your life, they gave you a home, and they haven't ever asked for anything in return. Like you said, it's rare for someone to give a gift without expecting something back.

Gifts always seem to come with strings, like the expectation of gratitude or obligation or reciprocity. My brother, John, likes to give gifts, but if you don't express gratitude enough, he gets so mad. He'll stomp around and huff and puff until you tell him how grateful you are for the pizza, movie, cupcake, etcetera.

Or, for instance, the Albany Hobdays were married twenty years ago. Allen (the Mr.) was so far in debt that he couldn't afford an engagement ring. So Uncle Morty Hobday paid off his debts. Allen paid Uncle Morty back in less than a year, but he's never, ever, ever let the Albany Hobdays or anyone else forget what he did. Now, whenever Uncle Morty needs something, he asks the

Albany Hobdays for a favor, "to pay him back for his generosity."

So that's why I think your hermit brothers are decent people. It doesn't seem like they are holding anything over you. They don't have any expectations either.

That's how I'd like to live my life. I've been thinking about this a lot. If I'm lucky enough to be able to do something for someone, I don't ever want to expect anything in return. Not even gratitude. Not anything. It'll be freely given.

And if I'm even luckier to love someone? Well. I'm going to give it freely. I won't hold it over them or use it as a threat or a bargaining chip. I won't expect gratitude or for them to love me back. I'm just going to give my love.

Because, you know, even someone like me wants to love.

I'll be thinking about you this year. Up there in the forest. In the quiet. Maybe you could read more books about furry-footed creatures and their loyal bearded friends? Or maybe you'll think about life and decide what's next for you.

I have a strong belief that us humans have to have a purpose to live well. And the more noble a purpose, the better we feel. For a long time, I wasn't sure I'd be around long enough to figure out my purpose. But then, this summer, I finally found it.

You see, I've spent a disproportionate amount of time in a hospital. And in retirement homes. Oh, and hospice. You might think, oh, you want to be a doctor! No. Not at all. I want... I want to be the reason someone's face lights up with joy when they're in a white room, surrounded by four walls, scared and alone. I saw that joy, and I even felt it in myself.

It was when someone walked in with a beautiful bouquet. An armful of bright, cheery sunflowers. A basket of hope-filled Gerbera daisies. A bouquet of sweet-smelling roses. There is something about flowers that lifts a person's soul. There are so many words that can't be spoken that can be shared through flowers. For instance: I love you, I'm with you, I miss you, feel better, I'm sorry, I'm here.

Flowers were the one thing that brought sun into a lonely room. That's what I want to do. I want to bring sunshine to people. So I'm studying floral design. Someday, I'll start my own business. What do you think of that?

You are the first person I've told. And you're the first person I've sent a flower to.

Have you found it already? Can you smell it on the paper?

It's from an antique rose bush that grows along our front fence. The bush was planted right after the house was finished. Now it's five feet tall and just as wide. In the summer, there are what seems like a hundred deep red pompoms blooming on the bush. It's so fragrant and sweet. There are always dozens of bees flying around it.

I dried these petals in the pages of my journal. They were creased between a line of wax paper and the months of July and August. Maybe you'll put the petals on your shelf, next to the cardinals. You can smell them whenever the woodstove leaks smoke. Hopefully they haven't crumpled to dust by the time they reach you.

Back in August, my family took a trip to the Grand Canyon. Have you ever been? It made me feel very small. Very insignificant. It's the same feeling I get when I look up at the stars. A sort of wondrous awe.

But then I think, aren't each of us as wondrous as a star? As unique and complex as the Grand Canyon?

While my whole family talked excitedly, pointing out crevices and terrifying drops, I was thinking, I wonder if Lee would like it here?

Would you? Have you been? What *do* you like? What's your favorite food? Your favorite song? Your favorite season? You asked your hermits if they believe in God, but do you?

I do. Not because I was raised Catholic, although I guess that's part of it. I've never told anyone this. But when my heart stopped years ago, I heard a voice. It was outside of me but inside me at the same time. I was terrified. I thought I was dying. The voice said, "All is well." That's all. But when I heard it, I wasn't afraid anymore. I felt at peace. I felt loved. I suppose I always thought that it was God who spoke to me. Do you think God talks to people? Maybe he's talking to us all the time, and it's only in the direst moments that we actually listen. I don't know.

Maybe we listen more at Christmas too.

Maybe at Christmas, our hearts are more open.

I have to go now. I can hear them calling my name upstairs. Soon, someone will flick on the basement light and shout down the stairs. Christmas Eve Eve dinner is ready. I'm not certain if it will be edible. Your guess is as good as mine.

I'll light a candle for you this year.

I've saved it for last, but I've been saying it in my heart this entire letter.

Merry Christmas, Lee. Merry Christmas.

I'm wishing you a very Merry Christmas.

I'm with you. I've been with you for three years now.

Just think, every night we look up at the same moon, and every once in a while we look up and watch the same snowfall.

I hope you write again. I hope you aren't upset I tried to find you. I think we're friends for a reason.

Yours,
    Cordelia

~

Cordelia Hobday
    1621 Tenderfoot Lane
    Romeo, NY

Dear Cordelia,

I know it's past Christmas but I wanted to reply. Thank you for trying to find me. I think I would've liked to meet you, although I'm also glad we didn't cross paths. I guess it's better this way. I can keep writing without feeling self-conscious.

I'm alright. You don't need to worry about me. I guess you know that if someone cares then they worry, and I can't tell you not to care, all I can say is, I'm used to taking care of myself, so don't worry.

I remember the snowfall, it was the only time it *really* snowed the whole month I was in New York. I like that you were there for it too.

I had my birthday. It's New Year's Day. Did I tell you

that? It's the only reason I remember it. I have a vague memory of wearing a New Year's hat and having a chocolate birthday cake when I was three years old. Saul made me a bear carved from wood and Jackson gave me a hunting rifle. I guess you were right. They care, don't they?

So thank you. Thanks for coming to New York. Thanks for the flowers. Thanks for letting me know you believe in God. I don't know if it was him talking to you or if it was a hallucination, I guess you can believe whatever you want. Up here, in the quiet, I think it's easier to hear God. The shifting of snow, the creak of the wind through the woods, the deer stripping bark from the trees. Maybe you're right, maybe humans are too loud, too busy to listen.

Did you know that in real life I think I've lost the ability to speak? I'm lucky to be able to get an avalanche of words out on the page to you.

My favorite food is currently chocolate yule log. I finally tasted the cake in New York and I can't get the flavor out of my head. I taste it in my dreams. Is that strange? The chocolate, the fudge frosting, the dark chocolate flakes.

My favorite season is autumn. It's cool enough to sleep outside. The days are still long and the sun slants so that everything has a gold sheen. It also has the best smells, fallen leaves, wet tree bark, and tart apple cider. I could eat apples all day. I'd argue that freshly picked Honeycrisp apples are the best tasting fruit in the whole world. If you walk through an orchard, you can smell the cidery fermenting tint of the fallen apples, the green scent of tall grass and clover, and the sweet ripeness of apples still on the tree. There is a sort of low buzz from the hundreds of worker bees that vibrates through your chest. And that Fall light falls down over your bare head, heating your skin. What do you think? Have I convinced you autumn is the best season?

My favorite song? I guess, I like "Silent Night." Not that I love silence so much that I have to have it in a song title, but because I remember it from before, the before I don't remember. Every time I hear the opening melody I get a sort of tight ball lodged in my chest. I don't know. Maybe it's not my favorite. Maybe it's my least favorite. Could be the same thing.

I've been to the Grand Canyon. I did like it and I know exactly what you mean. Someday you should go to Banff. I think you'll like it there even more. There are wild roses in Banff that were blooming the summer I went through. They're dark pink with yellow centers and they crop up in the most unlikely places, like at the edge of a mountain lake, peeking up at the sun.

The rose petals arrived only slightly crumpled. I can still smell their fragrance. We don't have roses in the balsam woods. I'll smell them whenever Saul is cooking lima bean stew or when Jackson throws too many wet logs on the fire.

I'm glad you found your purpose. Although you didn't ask, I know you'll succeed. I think I'll spend the year deciding where to go next. What to do.

By the way, how old are you? Can I ask that? I know people say you aren't supposed to ask a woman her age, but I'm not sure that counts in this scenario. I thought you were about eighty, but seeing as you were sitting in a laundry sink hiding in the dark, I'm not so sure anymore.

Happy New Year.

Lee

≈

Dear Lee,

Happy Birthday! I'm 17, almost 18. For the next two months, we're the same age. I sent a pack of brownies. It's not chocolate yule cake, but I made them myself.

By the way, my favorite season is winter. I love the clear night skies, the first snowfall, the smell of evergreen (if it's real!), warm mittens, crackling fires, the sound of ice skates on a frozen pond, and the taste of hot chocolate with peppermint after sledding all afternoon.

My favorite song is "Don't Go Breaking My Heart." It started as a joke, but then I started to like it, then I started to love it and now it's my favorite.

My favorite food is mashed potatoes with roasted garlic and melted butter on top. But I agree, there is a special place for chocolate yule cake.

Happy Birthday. I won't forget it. Enjoy the brownies. Don't tell me if they're terrible. I worked hard on those!

Yours,
  Cordelia

≈

Cordelia,

Seventeen?!!! 17? I thought you were *old*.

By the way, the brownies were the best I've ever had.

—Lee

~

Dear Lee,

Thanks. Here's another batch. I added chocolate chips this time.

Yours,
    Cordelia

~

Cordelia,

I've adjusted my favorite food. It's your brownies. Stay my friend forever or I'll end up a drifter wandering the globe in search of brownies as good as yours.

—Lee

∾

Dear Lee,

I can send the recipe?

Yours,
  Cordelia

∾

Cordelia,

I don't want the recipe. I want you to make them for me. By the way, stop writing me. We're only supposed to send Christmas cards and it's nearly February. Oh. Which means it's almost your birthday. Happy Birthday Cordelia. I sent a rose I carved. It's terrible, I know, but Saul is helping me with woodworking and he says I have promise (beyond the cheap wood ornaments I can make). Talk to you in December.

—Lee

∾

Dear Lee,

Thank you for the rose.

I thought it was a hamburger, so I'm glad you told me it was a rose. Just kidding.

And it wasn't me that kept writing. It was you.

Thank you for the present. I do love it. It's small enough for me to keep in my pocket.

By the way, if you need me, you can write any time. You don't have to wait until Christmas.

Yours,
Cordelia

seven years ago

7

———

Seven Years Ago

Cordelia Hobday
　　1621 Tenderfoot Lane
　　Romeo, NY

Dear Cordelia,

Merry Christmas.

I spent months thinking about writing you but I never could manage to pick up a pencil and a piece of paper. But now Christmas is here, and I have to put to paper the words I've been avoiding. They've been all tangled up inside, impossible to unknot, but here they are.

Saul died in March.

You can't tell, but I just spent five minutes staring at

the paper before I could write that down. I'm gripping the pencil so tight I think it might snap in half. Why is it so hard? I guess you already know. He was one of the only people in the world I've ever cared about and who ever cared about me.

I never told him. He wasn't that kind of person. He didn't even like it when I said thank you. But that first year here, I talked enough. In all that talking, why didn't I ever say, you mean something to me. You're like the grandfather I always wished I had.

Once, when he nearly slipped on the ice, I grabbed his elbow to stop him from falling. He clapped me on the back in thanks. That was the most affection we ever showed. Otherwise, it was a silent nod at breakfast, a quiet drive hauling wood, a coffee in the yard watching the moon rise over the balsam fir.

You were right. Jackson and Saul cared for me.

I guess that's what I worry about. I know it now, even if they never said a thing. But did they know that I was grateful, that I cared about them too?

I guess Saul would say that it doesn't matter. Words don't mean a thing. But why is it then that I regret so much not speaking them?

Thank you. I'm grateful. You're the grandfather I always wanted.

It's too late, are, I think, the worst three words in the English language.

I thought it was quiet before, but even quiet people still create the sounds of living. With Saul gone, the cabin became as quiet as a tomb. I was seeped in grief and Jackson stewed in anger. Instead of sadness he decided to let anger consume him. It's not a surprise that on opening day of hunting season Jackson got stone cold drunk, passed out, and fell headfirst out of his deer blind. It was a twenty foot fall.

I'm sorry to write all this. I don't think it's anything you want to hear at Christmastime. And like I always told you, don't worry about me, I'm alright. I'm always alright.

No. Do you remember how we said we'd always be honest? I can't be honest about this during the day, but at night, Cordelia, there's this huge, black, yawning darkness that I swear is going to swallow me up, like I'll disappear, and I think, if only I could cry, it'd recede, and I'd be alright. But I've never cried. Not that I can remember. Not in my whole life. Maybe we all get an allotment of tears for our lifetime, and I already used mine all up. I guess I was too young to remember it. Or maybe tears are like words. Sometimes they're all tangled up and crammed inside you and they just get stuck and nothing you do can get them out.

I guess I'm not sure what to think. I don't want to look at it now. Do you remember how I said that I didn't like people in books because they whine or were in self-denial? I think denial is looking a little more attractive.

Anyway, let me tell you something happy. Let's see. There's a red squirrel who decided to befriend me. Every morning he skitters over the moss covered shingles of the cabin to wake me up. Then when I walk into the kitchen he hangs upside down like an acrobat from the molding over the kitchen window. He peers in, with these black, beady, mischievous eyes and then he chitters at me, like he's scolding me. I got sunflower seeds from the feed store and so after he yells at me I walk out and throw a spoonful of them onto the dirt. The squirrel, I named him Tom because I'm not going to eat him, has reddish brown fur, a soft white belly, and a bushy red tail with a black fur tip. His left ear has a notch in it, probably where an owl almost nipped him for dinner, and he likes to stand on his back two legs and alternately yell at me or shove sunflower seeds into his mouth.

To keep the quiet at bay, I have conversations with him. We've chatted about the books he likes (none), his favorite food (nuts and seeds), and his philosophy on life (live for today). Anytime I try to bring up leaving New Brunswick he gives me a condescending look and skitters away.

But I'm leaving. There isn't any reason to stay.

I was surprised when Stalwart Branch's only lawyer told me Jackson and Saul had left me the cabin and all the land. If I wanted, I could stay here in the quiet for the rest of my life. Carry on. Delivering wood. Feeding Tom. Receiving a card from you once a year.

But I can't. I think if I do stay, I really will be swallowed up by that darkness.

You have your family, your home, your flowers, your dreams. Me. You have me. I like the thought of you having me. Of being someone's.

I've been thinking about what I have. Is it necessary to have something or someone in this life? I have the cabin, the woods, a squirrel who is only loyal because of sunflower seeds. And I have you.

After nine months of not writing, when I wish I had, I don't want to regret not saying this. You are the friend I always wanted but never thought I deserved.

I care about you.

I don't care if we never meet. I don't care if I never know what you look like or if I never sit in the same room as you or if I never hear your voice. None of that would make me care anymore than I already do.

I care about you.

I guess I wanted to say that in case one of our hearts unexpectedly gives out while shoveling snow or one of us gets drunk and falls headfirst out of a deer blind or . . . I'll say it, you writing me is the best thing that ever happened to me. You're the best friend I've ever had.

I'll be 18 in two weeks. I'm leaving New Brunswick. The lawyer thinks he can help me get a real ID by tracking down my foster care records. I was in foster for about five minutes flat before I decided to jump the fence, metaphorically speaking. Anyway, when I have my ID I'll be leaving.

I've heard about an opportunity out in Iraq, driving supplies. Iraq is about as far away from New Brunswick as you can get. It'll be hot. Dry. I don't know if they have woods there full of fir trees. And I don't know if they have snow. But I need to get away.

I'll write you, but don't worry if my card is delayed next year. I promise I'll write. I'll be thinking of you. Don't worry, I'll keep your lucky penny in my pocket, it's kept me safe and given me a fair bit of luck so far.

I've been dreaming about your brownies. Maybe I could convince you to send me a package for Christmas. What did you do this year? Did you open your own flower shop? Are you still studying? Have you taken any more trips? What are you doing this Christmas?

Thinking about you, your funny, noisy family and your old overrun house, I'm smiling, and the truth is, it's my first smile in days. Weeks. I guess that's the sort of Christmas gift you give. I'm sorry I didn't write sooner, I feel lighter than I have in months. I forgot that that's what writing you does.

I've missed you. I know that doesn't make sense, but I

missed you. I hope your Christmas is as full of noise and burnt food as you described. Here's an idea. How about on Christmas Day at 10 p.m. we both go outside and look up at the North Star. Please tell me you can find the North Star. You find the Big Dipper, the two stars at the end of the handle point to the North Star. It's the big, bright one at the end of the handle on the Little Dipper. At 10 p.m. on Christmas, I'll be outside, looking at the North Star. I'll wish you Merry Christmas then. I'll say it out loud, and maybe you'll hear me. I'll be listening for you. But just in case you don't hear me, Merry Christmas, Cordelia. Merry Christmas.

—Lee

P.S. I included a drawing of Tom the Squirrel shoving his cheeks full of sunflower seeds. Also in early summer these purple-blue marsh violets bloom everywhere, they made me think of you. I pressed one for you and included it between the pages.

~

Lee Weston
    12933 E. Beaver Lake Road
    Stalwart Branch, NB
    Canada

Dear Lee,

I'm sorry.

I'm sorry about Saul and I'm sorry about Jackson. This is one of those times when words feel inadequate. When I wish that there were a new language, new words to describe what I want to say. But here I am constrained by twenty-six letters and the inadequacy of my ability to express them.

If I were with you, I would sit next to you, right under the boughs of the balsam firs. I'd hold your hand if you wanted, and I'd fill the silence for you. I'd talk about anything you wanted—the Christmas parade in Romeo, how a lightning bolt struck the roof this summer and set the shingles on fire, how I'm hopeless at floral design but I'm refusing to give up.

You wouldn't have to talk. You wouldn't have to cry. You wouldn't have to root through the pain or dig it up. You can keep it buried for as long as you like, and someday if you want, we can grab shovels and face it together. Sometimes it's easier to confront something painful if you know that there's someone with you. I'll be with you, if you like.

Until then, I'm sorry.

You said that you regret not telling Saul and Jackson that you cared. Trust me, they knew. Words aren't the only way we share what we feel. Humans are so much more complex than that. Did you ever meet someone and right away you liked them for no reason whatsoever? You didn't even have to say a word. You just knew. Or have you ever spent the most perfect hour with someone, yet when it's done, you realize you didn't really talk at all?

I promise. They knew. Please don't regret not telling them. I get the feeling that words didn't matter to them. It was you staying, keeping them company, hunting, working, cooking, just being there. I bet, if you think about it, they might say to you: thank you, you're the grandson we always wanted.

Trust me. This is coming from someone who knows.

When all the words run out (and they will, they do), what's left is just the comfort of someone you love, sitting next to you, holding your hand.

So right now, through this letter, I'm holding your hand.

You're right. You have me. I'm glad that you've claimed me. Mainly because I'm selfish, and I want to keep you as my friend forever.

I have to admit, I have reservations about you leaving for Iraq. It isn't because I want you to stay in New Brunswick. Because, let's be honest, your squirrel friend has no appreciation for books. But it's dangerous there. Won't you be driving through unstable areas? Won't you be risking your life?

I'm trying to say that I care about you. Please, no matter where you are, be careful. I want you to live a long life so I can keep sending you brownies (double chocolate chip this time), and you can keep sending me cheap wood ornaments carved by hand.

I'm old enough (in spirit at least) to know that you can't live someone else's life. There must be a good reason you're going, so I won't tell you to stay. I won't even ask you to come to Romeo.

Besides, John and his fiancée Kylie had a pipe burst. It flooded their first floor, so they're staying in the guest room down the hall with the ugly paisley wallpaper for the foreseeable future. That only leaves the attic, and like I said before, you wouldn't like living up there.

I think by next year I'll have my own apartment. I'm

still studying floral design and business at the local community college. It's about an hour away. I commute for classes, and I have an internship at a florist's about thirty miles from home. In my mind I imagined my internship going a lot differently than it has. See, I pictured crafting these gorgeous pink peony bouquets while soft classical music played in the background and customers browsed the dreamy, sweet smelling shop.

Ha!

Hahaha!

I'm only telling you this to make you smile. Otherwise I'd never share. Lee. I come home every night sweaty, smelly, red-faced, and sore. I spend early morning until late *lifting*.

I lift heavy buckets of water. I lift heavy chemical drums to treat the plants and keep them fresh. I lift shelves and racks of arrangements. I load the van. I unload the van. I clean out the flower cooler. I sweep. I mop. I dust. I run around like a maniac from the minute I arrive at work until the second I leave.

What don't I do? I don't arrange flowers. No, sir.

No.

I get pricked by prickers. I get poked by floral wire. I get chemical treatment spilled on me. I get sweaty. Sometimes I get covered in fishy stinky manure-y liquids. But I don't get to touch the flowers.

Me and Elizabeth, the other intern, sometimes mimic Mrs. Krantz, the florist.

"Interns do *not* design!"

We say that in high, pinched voices when we're in the back room lugging fifty-pound buckets across the floor. Then we start to laugh, and once we start, we can't stop.

Maybe I should be more upset about not making a

single arrangement during this internship. Except. I'm too darn tired. This internship is like the iron man triathlon of jobs.

In class, Elizabeth is the best designer. The instructors love her. They love me too. But only because I'm the worst designer, and somehow, I always illustrate perfectly what you aren't supposed to do.

I suppose, I'd say, *to hell with it all*, if I didn't want it so bad.

But if it makes you smile, I think that's worth it too. Picture me, too short, too scrawny, trying to lug a giant bucket of long-stem red roses across a concrete floor. Then I slip on some water. I fall on my butt and an open tub of Mrs. Krantz's "fish puree and manure juice" special treatment spills all over me. I'm dripping wet, stinky, soppy, and sweaty. And that's my day, swimming in the roses.

I hope you laugh. It makes me laugh. Even if I'm the worst designer in my class. Even if I'm stuck in Mrs. Krantz's boot camp for suckers. It makes me laugh.

Someday, I'll start my own shop. Elizabeth says she'll join me. We'll be a team and call our place For the Love of Flowers.

I want you to know I miss you too. It doesn't have to make sense. It can just be.

I didn't take any trips this year. I've been too busy with school and wowing people with my extreme lack of floral design skill. I'll get there. I promise.

Thank you for the violet petals. I love them. They're the prettiest blue. I wish I could bottle their scent. They smell almost like Valentine heart candies. Sweet and hopeful.

I bet you didn't realize that. Maybe you haven't even had those candies? You should. They are delicious.

Next Valentine's Day I'll send you some in the mail. Don't yell at me for sending you something outside of Christmas. I'm going to do it, no matter what you say. In fact, to tell you the truth, I write you every month of the year, even if I don't put it to paper.

You wanted to know what I'm doing for Christmas? The invasion of the Hobdays will begin any day now. My little cousin DeeDee is in *The Nutcracker*, so we'll be taking up half the auditorium to clap and cheer enthusiastically when she appears on stage.

My family is in charge of dinner this year. When my mom married my dad she made him promise in his vows that he'd never make her set foot in the kitchen. She loathes cooking. My dad doesn't know how to boil water.

So when I was about eight I got tired of microwave dinners and takeout (every day except Sunday). I took over meal-time. You should see me when I cook. I put on music. I sing. I chop. I'm fearless in the kitchen. I'll make anything at least once.

This Christmas I'm putting my siblings to work. We'll have a Christmas ham glazed in clover honey, mini brie pastry puffs with figs and apricots, butternut squash blossoms, homemade orange cranberry sauce, parmesan and garlic mashed potatoes, asparagus wrapped in pastry dough, fresh green beans with lemon zest and slivered almonds, butternut squash soup, and French rolls with homemade herby butter. I'm telling you the whole menu so you can taste it too.

Maybe you can imagine all us Hobdays crammed into the kitchen, the dining room, the living room, plates perched on our knees, trays, and tables. Sparkling juice or wine poured into plastic cups. Old china and paper plates interchangeable. Then for dessert, in honor of you, I'm making a chocolate yule log. You said it was your favorite. When I bite into it, I'll wish you a Merry Christmas.

And then at five minutes to ten, I'll run outside. Mittens, coat and hat on. I'll find the North Star. Of course I know how to find it! And I'll count down the seconds. I'll stamp my feet to keep them warm. I'll rub my hands together. I'll blow out puffs of air into the night cold. And up into the clear winter sky, I'll know. You're looking up. I'm looking up. We have each other.

I'll listen for you.

You listen for me.

Merry Christmas, Lee.

I care about you.

You're the friend I always dreamed of. Thank you for writing me. I hope you never stop.

Merry Christmas.

Yours,

Cordelia

P.S. I hope you liked the brownies. I keep adding more chocolate. I also included a picture I took of my home. It has all the Christmas lights up and the candles glowing in the windows. My dad put that atrocious plywood Santa and Reindeer in the front yard this year.

What do you think? Is it exactly like you imagined?

I thought you'd like to see it. If you're lonely, or missing me, or if you just need a little Christmas magic you can look at the window on the second floor. The third one to the right. That's my room. It's where I'm writing to you from. I'm there now. Thinking of you.

~

Dear Lee,

Happy New Year! Happy Birthday! Make a wish. This one will come true.

Yours,
　　Cordelia

~

Cordelia,

Thank you for the confetti and the music birthday card. I played it until the battery died, it made me laugh, and I laughed so hard that Tom ran off, startled and shouting at me, leaving half of his sunflower seeds behind.

I made a wish, but I think they say you aren't supposed to tell anyone what it is. You'll have to let me know if it comes true since it was a wish for you.

I stood outside, Christmas night, for a long time. I listened for you at ten, and I think I heard you. Or I felt you there.

By the way, I don't believe that you're the worst at floral design. It's not even remotely possible. Sometimes you can want something and no matter how much you want it, no matter how much you wish it, it won't ever happen. I've wished for the impossible enough times to know. You can't change facts. But you being the worst isn't a fact. It's just an opinion and I think it's a faulty one. I bet, when you make a design, it's got a bit of you in it and anything that has a bit of you is something special. I guess what I'm trying to say is, keep trying and the more you that you put in it, the better it'll be. Maybe someday I'll see one of your designs and I'll be proven right.

—Lee

P.S. Thank you for the brownies. I'll be careful, don't worry. You're right, I need to do this. Sometimes I think, it's that if I see enough of the world, someday I'll recognize home. I know it's not over there, but maybe it's somewhere between here and there, and in that unknown place, I'll find it.

~

Lee,

Happy Valentine's Day! Here are the candy hearts I promised. My favorite is the pink heart, which is supposed to taste like cherry. The yellow is supposedly banana, but I think it tastes like fruit cake. You might like it.

Yours,
    Cordelia

~

Cordelia,

It tastes nothing like fruit cake. By the way, happy birthday. It's your turn to make a wish. Make it a good one.

—Lee

six years ago

8

Six years ago

New York, NY
    December 1

Cordelia

The sun slipped below the Hudson River, and just like that, a perfect clear blue winter day became an even more perfect purple and gold-tinted winter night. The sky was clear and glossy, and *if* you could see the stars from Manhattan, this would be the night that it would happen.

Corey tilted her face toward the darkening sky and let herself smile. Today felt like magic. December was finally here and Christmas spun toward her in quickening pirouettes.

She felt it in the cold fingers of wind that pinched her cheeks. She smelled it in the evergreens lining the streets. She tasted it in the cinnamon sprinkled in her morning coffee.

New York was wrapped in ribbons and lights, and Christmas music played in the streets every time someone opened a shop door and let the music spill out.

On top of it all, she was in the city with her best friend (well, best friend that she'd met in real life), and they'd spent an entire week buried in flowers. She, quite literally, was in heaven.

Lee would write her soon. There was that. She wouldn't deny that every year at Thanksgiving the world started looking brighter, the air was filled with expectancy, and she was *happier*.

But more than that, she and Elizabeth would graduate in the spring. They'd finish their internship with Mrs. Kratnz. And then they'd start their shop, For the Love of Flowers.

There was the matter of funding. She'd been denied a small business loan by half a dozen banks already. But today, that hitch didn't matter.

Because it was a perfect night. In a perfect city. And Christmas was almost here.

They were in Chelsea, on the west side of Manhattan, nearing The Highline, where a frost-coated park full of shrubs and flowers and trees floated high above the city streets.

Much earlier, before the sun even peaked above the horizon, they'd been at the New York Flower Market on West 28th Street surrounded by piney evergreens, jewel red and emerald green poinsettias, and enough blooming amaryllises to make Corey's head spin.

There was the noise of diesel trucks delivering wholesale flowers and plants. The bright colors of red and white and green blossoms. The scent of so many evergreens. It was all so overwhelming. It filled her with expectation and hope and that particular Christmassy feeling that she could never quite describe.

"It was the mistletoe, wasn't it?" Elizabeth said dryly, lifting an eyebrow.

She peeked over at Corey with a twisty, funny smile. They were at a crosswalk, waiting for the light. The street was less busy than it had been earlier in the day. The tall brick and metal buildings were dimming their lights, closing up for the night. Past The Highline was a row of art galleries. But in the stretch of sidewalk where Corey and Elizabeth waited, there were only a few restaurants, bars, and a coffee shop to light the darkening street.

They were staying at a hotel only a few blocks down with the rest of their class. This was their one field trip for the year—a week at The Flower School. Twelve-hour days of classic design, avant-garde styling, and holiday techniques. But all that was over. The week was over and tonight was their last night in the city.

Corey's smile tilted higher, and she looked over at her best friend. "Mistletoe? I don't know what you mean."

Elizabeth snorted. She was almost always dry, sarcastic, or ironic. She had long wavy black hair, a full mouth, and a certain intangible allure, like an orchard in full bloom. Her arms and legs were covered in tattoos, mostly flowers that were more dangerous than they looked (for instance, the carnivorous Venus fly trap, or the poisonous oleander, or the thorny rose).

That was Elizabeth to a T. She was more spiky thorn than rose. It's why Corey liked her. Elizabeth was darkly funny, interesting, and nothing like herself. Like Elizabeth said, they went well together—like spiking grape juice with hemlock.

"It's obvious. You've finally realized that mistletoe is one of the most messed-up—yet entirely appropriate—symbols of love that humans have ever come up with."

Corey tapped her finger against her lip, fighting her smile. "Because?"

"It's ruthlessly parasitic. It digs into trees and sucks out their nutrients, eventually killing them. Beware mistletoe! One kiss and you're done."

"I like mistletoe."

"Of course you do, you're a romantic."

The light changed and they followed the flow of pedestrian traffic, turning north toward their hotel. Corey tugged her wool coat closer at a bit of wind, rushing westward from the Hudson.

She knew why Elizabeth thought she was a romantic. She wasn't one, but Elizabeth swore she was. It's because she never dated, never talked about dating, never . . . anything. Elizabeth thought she was saving herself for True Love (with capitals). After all, they lived in the soul mate capital of the world.

But really, Corey had given up on dating years ago when she realized that she wasn't going to find that connection, that understanding she was looking for.

She had a connection with Lee, but she was too practical to think that the connection they had would cross the fragile boundary from paper to real life. She wasn't certain it would, and so far, she was too scared to ask him if he wanted to find out.

"I'm not a romantic. I just like parasitic plants. Like . . . hmm . . . my favorite. The stinking corpse lily."

Elizabeth choked on a laugh.

"The yellow rattle. The ghost plant. Oh! The Australian Christmas Tree—"

"Stop!"

"Kiss me. I'm a mistletoe! I'll suck the life from you and . . . I know him."

Corey stopped walking and stared into the warm yellow glow of a large window. It was a bar. One of the small, crowded, noisy places tucked away all throughout the city. The front was glistening wood, curved and rounded, set along wide windows. Through the glass, the white and yellow light spilled into the night, inviting passersby into the warmth.

"You know the Santa?" Elizabeth asked, eyeing the Santa not ten feet away, ringing a bell for charity.

"No. I know him."

Corey pointed through the window at the tall figure at the wooden bar. The small bar was crowded, packed shoulder to shoulder. Even outside Corey could hear the loud rumble of conversation leaking through the glass and under the wooden door. She was surprised she'd noticed him at all.

But it *was* him.

She could see the left side of his face reflected in the bar's mirror. He was turned away from her, looking at something across the bar with a half-smile on his face. It's the smile that did it. It twisted her stomach and made her heart flutter violently against her rib cage.

"The bald guy in the bow tie drinking the sidecar?"

"The tall, black-haired one." Corey unconsciously took a step forward, toward the bar door.

"Him?" Elizabeth stepped to the window and peered in.

They were standing at the glass now, Peeping Toms looking in at the joviality and noise of a full bar on a Friday night.

He hadn't changed much. He was still tall, lean, dark. His face was a little sadder. His brown eyes a little more opaque and hard to read. He looked lonelier, and even as young as he was, there were a few weathered lines on his face.

He still had that wild, untamed aura. And even though Corey knew he wasn't Lee, she still thought of this man as something uncivilized and outside the boundaries of her four walls. Maybe it was in the way he stood, as if he was aware of everything around him, and could act in an instant. Or maybe it was the muscles bunched at his shoulders or the coiled strength so obvious, even when he was sitting still.

"That man? The kiss like an angel, make love like the devil man? Him?"

His eyes flicked to the mirror, and in that instant, Corey was swallowed in his gaze. She tumbled forward and she remembered the promise of snowfall, the smell of evergreen, the taste of chocolate yule log, and the feel of falling in love at first sight.

She'd thought that, hadn't she?

It'd been two years, but she felt it again.

She felt like she'd swallowed a whiskey in one desperate gulp and her body was burning with it. Glowing and fiery. She was dazed, knocked breathless by the sight of him.

Was this what she'd been waiting for? This connection?

"I'm going in."

"What? Into the bar? Corey, you're—"

"I'll see you back at the hotel. Don't wait up."

And then, ill-advised or not, Corey walked into the heat, the noise, and the crowd to say hello.

Corey slid onto the barstool next to him, the wood of the seat warm and smooth. She was surprised that the stool was empty, considering the bar was so tightly packed that it'd taken minutes to squeeze and push her way from the door to the counter.

The acoustics bounced sound from ceiling to brick and plaster walls and off the wood floor so that all the sounds merged into an avalanche of conversation. Her ears were already ringing.

This many bodies crammed together gave off enough heat to fire up a furnace, so she gladly stripped off her wool coat, pulled free her hat and mittens, and then unwound her scarf. Since the stool didn't have a back, she set them all in her lap, and then perched there, waiting for him to notice her.

He didn't.

It was almost like he was sitting in a forested glade, all by himself, just watching the cardinals hop from branch to branch and the shadows flicker over the boughs. He was that removed from the noise of it all.

Corey wanted to pop the bubble around him and shake him into noticing her.

She did the next best thing.

She held out her hand, sticking it over his plate of burger and fries, and thrusting it practically under his nose. He couldn't miss it.

"Chris. Chris like Christmas." She smiled at him. She

couldn't help it. Her whole body was smiling as she leaned toward him. What were the chances of running into him again? One in a million. Less.

He blinked. Looked down at her hand and then at her. His eyebrows pulled down and his forehead wrinkled. It was obvious he didn't remember her and she almost lost her smile, but then he blinked and the confusion that clouded his face cleared.

Chris turned toward her, moving his body so that she was shielded from the noise and the bumping elbows of the crowd. His brown eyes lit up as he took in her cold, wind-bitten cheeks, tangled red hair, and wide grin.

"It's you." He said this slowly, with that deep, rockslide rumble she remembered.

"It's me. Corey."

Her grin widened, and in response, his mouth tilted up at the edges until he was smiling just as wide as she was. For some reason she very much wanted to hug him. It didn't make any sense, but she felt as if she'd been waiting years to see him again and she'd only just realized it. Then his eyes flicked to her mouth and her whiskey-fired blood started burning again, and suddenly, she very much wanted to do more than hug him.

Which was . . . unexpected.

She cleared her throat. He took her extended hand and shook it, that happy light still in his eyes. She wasn't surprised when tingles raced up her palm and knocked her heart around.

"I saw you from outside." She had to nearly shout this. The bar was as loud as a jet plane taking off with the music, the people, the TVs, and the blenders. "Are you selling trees again?"

He wrinkled his brow again and leaned closer. It was obvious he couldn't hear her.

"Are you selling trees this year, Chris like Christmas?"

He shook his head. "Not trees . . . not . . . name—"

She couldn't hear him either. It was hopeless.

But all the same, he was looking at her expectantly, so she nodded and smiled.

He said something else, but the bar was so loud that she couldn't even catch a single word. She gave him a hopeless look and held up her hands in defeat.

He looked around the bar, took in the noise and crowd, and got a frustrated line between his brows. Then Corey did something she thought she would never do, something that she'd never even considered doing. She leaned close. Her arm brushed his, her hand rested on the edge of the bar inches from his. Their pinkies almost touching. This close, she could smell him over the beer and liquor and fried food scent of the bar. He was evergreen and snow and clear night skies. She felt a happy flip in her belly.

Then she squeezed her eyes closed, curled her toes in her boots, and asked with her mouth close to his ear, "Do you want to go somewhere?"

When she opened her eyes he'd pulled back and was studying her face.

She knew what she looked like. She could see herself in the mirror. She was flushed and blushing. Her pale skin was red and her hair was a tangled mess. Her long-sleeved shirt was one she wore to lug tubs of flowers in, so it had holes in it, stains, and was just this side of too worn out to even use for a dusting rag. Her jeans were full of holes too, but she'd put on long johns beneath them. She hadn't come to New York to dress up and dine at expensive restaurants. She'd come to work, to get dirty, and to learn.

But now, she wished she'd at least had a clean shirt on.

She was hot, flushing under his solemn gaze. It's as if he was looking right into her. As if he knew her. Almost like she felt she knew him.

Finally, after a long, thoughtful silence, he nodded, and the tight ball in her belly unknotted.

"Alright."

He flagged the bartender. Put bills on the counter. And then they were moving through the mass of bodies. And while it had taken her long minutes to make the twenty feet between door and bar, it took only seconds with him cutting through the crowd. She followed close, keeping in his wake.

And then they were outside.

The cold hit her, splashing over her with an invigorating chill. She blinked up at the clear sky—still no stars. The silence fell over her as soon as the door swung shut behind them. Her ears rang, adjusting to the relative quiet. There were just a few taxis driving past, their tires hissing on the pavement. A group of friends across the sidewalk hurrying to a restaurant. A mother and son walking a dog. It *was* quiet.

The Highline was visible through the metal and glass buildings. The trees and bushes glowed in the luminescence of the street lamps, like a cloud island floating in the sky.

She stepped closer to Chris, and he looked down at her with an expectant, somewhat surprised smile. To her, it said, isn't fate funny?

"I saw you from outside. When I was walking past."

She gestured at the bar. She wasn't sure if he'd heard her before. "I didn't expect to see you again. Are you selling trees this year?"

She tilted onto her toes and back down again, rocking a bit in the growing cold. She'd slid her coat and scarf back on, but just like last time, Chris was only in a thick flannel, faded jeans, and leather boots.

All the same, she could feel the heat and the warmth of him.

"No. I'm . . . just moving through. I'm only here until tomorrow."

He tilted his head then looked down at her. They stared at each other in silence for a moment. It wasn't awkward like other silences Corey had known. Not like the silence her family had when they learned she needed another surgery. That was a scared silence. Not the silence her parents had when she was little and she'd done something wrong. That was a disappointed silence. Nor was it an angry silence or a judging silence.

No.

This was a wonderful silence.

One full of expectation and maybe . . . magic.

It felt a bit like magic.

"Have you been looking for another ugly tree?"

Corey laughed and shook her head. "Not yet. Soon, though. I hope . . . have you eaten any more chocolate yule logs?"

Chris smiled, and it looked like he was reliving feasting on that last yule log they'd shared on the sidewalk. "Not since you and I shared one."

They were quiet again, smiling at each other. Then a taxi honked from down the block and Corey shook out of the glowy feel that was slowly folding over her.

"Do you want to walk?" She hoped he did.

He could ask where. He could ask why. Instead he nodded.

They headed northeast toward the glowing spire of the Empire State Building. It was a spiral of red and white and beckoned them like a bright Christmas beacon.

Corey hadn't put her mittens or hat on, and the cold was biting at her fingers. After thirty seconds of do-it-don't-do-it-do-it tug-of-war with herself, she reached over and gently brushed her hand against Chris's.

"Cold?" He looked over and wrapped her hand in his.

She was done. She knew it. She was a goner.

She knew enough about love to realize that this was it. Hadn't she grown up in a house where her parents were in love? Hadn't both her siblings fallen in love and gotten married? Didn't she live in a town where love was practically pumped into the water supply?

It didn't matter that they hadn't spoken more than a dozen words. Maybe three dozen in the few times they'd met. Like she'd written to Lee—you didn't always need words to *know*.

They walked down the sidewalk, wending northeast, deep into the heart of the city. The sky had shaded from purple and gold to a deep indigo. There was a universe out there, expansive and mysterious. But weren't people the same? Didn't they each have a universe just as expansive and mysterious inside them?

Maybe that was why people needed to love. Because if they didn't, they'd be a universe, alone, floating into nothingness. Maybe that was why when you found someone to love, you wanted to keep them by your side.

Corey looked over at Chris. All these thoughts

clogged up her chest, making it impossible to say, well, anything at all.

But it seemed he didn't mind the quiet. He was comfortable and relaxed next to her. His stride easy, and his hand warm around hers.

But when the silence had gone on too long for her, Corey took a breath to clear out the words in her throat.

"I don't usually do this." She peered up at him. He was still tall, the top of her head just reaching his shoulders.

"Do what?" He gave her a funny smile. He knew. He knew *exactly* what.

She smiled back. "This. Talk to random strangers. Invite them to go somewhere. Hold their hand."

She jostled her hand, now warm in his, to prove the point.

"If you did, then it wouldn't be special, would it?"

She stared at him. That was exactly it. This felt special.

"Besides, we aren't strangers. We've bonded over ugly trees and chocolate yule log."

She laughed. "You're right. Absolutely. My other hand is still cold. Do you . . ."

He chuckled, shifted her to the opposite side of him, and grabbed her other hand, warming it in his.

"I really love New York at Christmas, don't you?" She waited for his answer.

He studied her expression for a moment, then asked, "Why do you love it?"

"Oh, I don't know. I love Christmas everywhere. But as soon as December hits, something shifts in the air. Like, well, like a wind is blowing in all the wonderful, exciting things that you've kept boxed away and have just been waiting to unwrap. All of a sudden, strangers are friends. Do you notice that? There's just kindness and generosity floating in the air, like . . . like mistletoe." She smiled at that, and then squeezed his hand. "And all you have to do is stand under it, and you'll . . . your heart will open. The bright lights, the wreaths and Christmas trees, the carolers singing, the bells, the cinnamon and peppermint, and . . . I love it all. And even more, at Christmas, did you ever notice the old songs, they always talk about coming home for Christmas, or returning to that person you love, or finding them . . . it's hope. Christmas is hope. And in New York, you see it all around you. Every corner there's a Christmas tree stand, or a bell ringer, or a window lit up and glowing. It's hope. It's friendship. Maybe, it's . . ." she trailed off.

Chris had stopped walking, and he was staring down at her with an unnamable expression on his face. It was as if he recognized her, or recognized what she was saying. And then she realized that she knew exactly what his expression was. It was loneliness. She'd seen it in the mirror when she watched him through the window. It was yearning. She'd felt it enough to know it.

"Are you alright?" She squeezed his hand.

"I'm always alright." He gave her a half smile, but she could see behind the warm brown of his eyes to the truth of the words. He wasn't always alright. But he was alright right now.

"I'm glad. I'm alright too. No, I'm better than alright. I just walked across Manhattan and saw all the lights and glitter. And I bullied a near-stranger into keeping my hands warm."

"You keep saying we're strangers, but every time you do, I feel like we aren't strangers at all."

She leaned close and smiled at him. "Here. I'll tell you a secret. If we share secrets we won't be strangers."

He cleared the smile from his face and gave her a grave, solemn look meant to acknowledge the seriousness of secret-sharing.

She laughed and knocked her shoulder against his, and he fought to keep the serious look on his face.

"Here it is. I hate, absolutely loathe the fact that I barely top five feet tall."

He lifted his eyebrows. "That's a secret? Your deep, dark secret?"

She snorted. "No. This is. Sometimes servers will think I'm a little kid, so I let them and I order off the kids menu. Because I love chicken nuggets dipped in honey and drinking chocolate milk out of a straw."

He laughed. She knew he couldn't help it. But he laughed. "Chicken nuggets?"

She nodded. "And then, I feel bad for lying, so I admit my age and pay the adult price."

He laughed harder at that. Then he held his hand to his heart and vowed, "Your deep, dark, devious secret is safe with me."

"Your turn. You have to tell me one now."

He fell quiet. Around them, even though they were close to the bustle of Herald Square, it felt as if the city went quiet. The breeze tugged at her, cold and crisp. She stepped closer, certain he was about to share something profound.

Finally, he nodded and smiled at her.

"A secret. I . . . I . . . like you. I don't know why. But I like you. And I kept the gold foil from the yule log box, and two years later I still have it. Because . . .I guess . . .because when I look at it, it makes me smile. That was

. . ." He shook his head. "That was too much of a secret, wasn't it?"

"No." She gripped his hand. "No. Not at all." She swallowed the lump in her throat and pushed at the knot of all the words she'd been unable to say.

"Actually, I have another secret. When I saw you, I felt like . . ." She was scared again and couldn't quite say the word. Love. "I felt like it was fate."

She waited for him to laugh.

He didn't.

Instead, he nodded toward the tall gray windowed building behind them. There was a large green canopy, two glass rotating doors, and a marble lobby.

"That's my hotel. I'm . . . that's where I'm staying."

"Oh." Corey's shoulders deflated. Was this it, then? Was he going up now? And they wouldn't see each other for another two years? Or ever?

Maybe they'd never see each other again.

She looked down at the gray concrete of the sidewalk. Flinched as a horn sounded. When she looked back up she realized that she was still holding his hand. But she was gripping it more tightly than before.

He gave her a hesitant smile. His black hair, thick and shaggy, was tousled by the wind. His eyes were dark and searching, and his face, some might call it hard, or even cold, but she didn't think so. He had a way of looking at her that made her warm, and happy, and seen.

She didn't want tonight to end.

"Can I come up?"

She held her breath while she waited for his answer.

Her lungs were burning when he finally asked, "You're sure?"

When she let out a relieved exhale, she realized what he was asking.

Are you sure?

Do you want to?

He was asking about what she'd felt since the second she sat down next to him. The awareness. The stretching tautness between them. The hum that vibrated deliciously over her skin every time her side whispered against his. He was asking about the thrum of expectancy that lapped over her and was winding itself in a tight coil in her abdomen, glowing and pulsing, waiting for him to hold her. More.

If she went up they wouldn't just talk.

She knew this.

There was a hungry, yearning, soulful ache inside her. She didn't know where it came from or why. She only knew that she didn't want the night to end. Not yet.

"I'm sure."

He smiled then, but it wasn't the smile she'd expected. It was shy, hesitant, happy.

She smiled back and clasped his hand.

Corey barely saw the bright white marble glow of the lobby. She didn't hear the doorman's greeting or her footsteps on the polished stone floor. She didn't smell the spicy cinnamon sticks tied with ribbons hanging from the Christmas tree in the lobby. She definitely didn't hear the tinkling of a piano playing Christmas carols.

She was only aware of the hard throb of her heart beating a strange, pulsing rhythm. It echoed through her, a drum in her ears. She hadn't felt her heart beat so insistently in years. It was almost as if it was trying to beat so hard that Chris would be able to hear it too.

The throb of it whirred through her blood and soon she was tingling all over. Or maybe that was the warmth of the lobby, bringing a flush to her cold skin. She concentrated on the feel of Chris's hand engulfing hers. The solid strength of his grip. The calluses on his palm and the tips of his fingers. The heat of him.

Every sense was attuned to him. As if the small point of contact between their hands spread across and feathered over her entire body. She was dizzy with it.

Then they were in the elevator. The brass and mirrors surrounded them. The panel lights ticked up, up, up, with a soft chime for each floor. The quick slide upward lifted her stomach and flipped it over.

They were quiet. Still holding hands. In the small confines of the elevator, the awareness prickled, tingled, and grew until Corey felt as if she might come apart, fall into a million pieces if she couldn't touch him. Press her mouth to his.

Their eyes caught and held in the glossy brass of the door. And then the elevator stopped and the doors slid open, pulling their reflections apart.

"I'm at the end of the hall."

She nodded.

They walked down a long hallway, wallpapered and thickly carpeted. All the sounds were muted by the carpet and the thick wood molding. There were gilded mirrors and beautifully fragrant floral arrangements of scented eucalyptus, ivory rose buds, white cushion poms, and baby's breath tucked in pine sprigs.

Any other time, Corey would linger and deconstruct in her mind the artistry of the arrangement. But now, she barely noticed the flowers over the press of his hand in hers.

Chris unlocked his door. The wood whispered over the carpet as he pushed it open. Then they were inside his hotel room.

They paused at the threshold.

The lights were off. The room was dim and golden. Small. There was a large bed with a plush white comforter and thick pillows. A navy-and-gold runner at the bottom of the bed matched the starry-skied pattern of the pillow shams.

Corey was sure there was more to the room—a wooden desk, a chair, a closet and bathroom, a coffee maker—but she could only focus on the bed. Beyond it was a wide window, the blinds open. The dark night sky and the lights of the city splayed out before them. That's where all the stars were. They were caught in the windows of apartment buildings and glowing from the lit-up tips of skyscrapers.

She looked back to Chris. He was quiet. An uncertain curl to the edge of his mouth.

"I'm going to do something, it's maybe a little crazy," Corey said, "but it feels right. It feels like if I don't kiss you—" When she said kiss you his eyes widened imperceptibly and then he swallowed and unconsciously bit his lower lip. "I'll . . . I'll . . ." She gave him a helpless look. "I'll have missed the one chance I had at . . ."

Why was it so hard to express what her heart was beating so wildly about? Why was it so difficult to put it into words?

"I don't want to miss you," she said, which didn't really make any sense at all, but it was how she felt.

But then he smiled, his mouth widening, and she knew he understood.

"I know exactly what you mean."

At the acknowledgment in his expression, Corey stood on her tiptoes and touched her mouth to his.

Her lips barely feathered over his. It was a soft, questing exhale. A snowflake melting in the sun. Her mouth caressed the warmth of his lips. He shivered under her and his hand shook in hers. His pained exhale echoed exactly what she felt. His mouth on hers was pain and pleasure. Need and denial. Passion and aching restraint. The light touch of his mouth sang and quivered inside her.

He gently let the warmth and wet of his mouth glide over hers. She made a small noise and he pulled her lips into his, stroking and caressing. She let go of his hand and gripped his shoulders, lifting and straining toward him.

His kiss was soft, searching, gentle and worshipful. He stroked her cheeks and brushed his fingers over her skin. He made noises, low humming sounds that vibrated through her. They were exploring. Diving into the unknown of each other. He kissed her, held her like she was precious. Infinitely valued. In the taste and gentle stroking of his mouth, she felt as if she'd known him for a lifetime.

They had the whole night to taste and to kiss. He pressed his lips over hers, angel feather light. She shivered as his mouth pulled her deep into a space where there was only the next exhale, the next stroke, the next slide of his tongue over her lips.

All thought fled. There was only feeling and need. There was only the next breath. The next kiss.

Then the kiss changed.

It was the sound she'd made. The need. The way she gripped his shoulders. Bit the edge of this lip. It unleashed a flood. An avalanche.

She wanted more of him. She didn't want just mouths and fingertips. She wanted everything.

Suddenly, she was in his arms. Her legs wrapped around his middle, and he gripped her thighs. Her back hit the door, and the breath thrust out of her. She clung to him and kept her mouth on his.

She rocked against him, and he let out a sharp, pained noise. She bit his lip again, and he hit his hand against the wall, splaying his fingers, pressing her between the door and his searching mouth. She was glowing. She was burning. She needed to touch him everywhere.

"Off." She could barely get the word out. His mouth was on hers and her breath came in short, quick gasps. "Off."

She pushed at his flannel, then tried to pry off her coat.

He pulled back. His eyes were dazed. His pupils were so dilated the black nearly swallowed the brown. His chest expanded in hard, quick breaths.

"You want—"

"Yes. *Yes.*"

"You're sure?"

She'd never been so sure of anything in her life.

"I want to make love. With you."

She barely got out the last bit. He was kissing her again. The heat of him, the clear winter sky scent of him wrapped around her. There was a hollow, empty ache inside her that was warming, and filling, and she needed him.

She tore at his flannel. He set her down, pushed her coat free. She shed her stained, torn shirt. Kicked off her boots. He dropped his flannel to the ground. He grasped her hips, ringed his calloused hands around her waist, and then pushed her jeans and long johns down in one ragged exhale. And she was nearly naked. Standing in front of him in underwear and a bra.

For years, she'd wondered if when she finally made love the small surgery scars on her chest would result in awkwardness. Not for her, but for whoever saw them. But the light was so dim, the dark blanketing them, that she was only feathered and outlined by the golden city lights. The telltale signs of her heart surgeries were hidden in the moment. Disappeared and unrecognizable. Just another contour of flesh and naked skin.

Chris stood still. Struck by the sight of her.

"You're beautiful. You're so beautiful." His voice was a quiet, aching rumble.

Corey looked at the muscled line of his chest. His tanned skin. The dark hair trailing to the button of his jeans. His chest was wide. His stomach taut. He held himself completely still.

She was overwhelmed by the sight of him.

She reached up, unclasped her bra, and let it drop to the floor.

"My heart. It's beating so hard." Her heart crashed around her chest. A throbbing, aching drum. Would it give out? Was this how she'd go? Death by pleasure?

At her words Chris's mouth lifted into a half smile. He stepped closer, then knelt in front of her. He dropped to his knees and took her waist in his hands. Then slowly he pressed his lips to the curve of her left breast.

"Here?"

She shook her head. His mouth scalded her.

He moved his lips lower. He trailed them over her nipple.

"Here?"

She shook her head. She was burning. Everywhere his mouth touched lit on fire.

She took his face in her hands. Sent her fingers over the stubble lining his jaw. She buried her hands in his thick, smooth black hair. Then he let her guide his mouth to the pounding of her heart.

"Here." She pressed his mouth to the insistent beat.

His lips lingered there. The warmth of his mouth soothing the fluttering. His hands spread across her, stroking her ribs and the underside of her breasts as his mouth pressed kisses to her thudding heart.

"I feel it." He looked up at her, his mouth at her breast.

She nodded, her skin hot and aching.

"Mine is beating hard too." He took her hand and rested it against his chest.

He was right. She could feel the thick, hard, quick beat of his heart.

At that acknowledgment Corey stepped back and pushed her underwear free.

The warm room air swirled around her. A flush prickled over her skin as she breathed in the snowy, clear night scent of him.

He stood before her and fumbled with the button on his jeans, his hands shaking. She tried to help him but was so urgent that she only made it worse. They kissed and laughed as they struggled to free him. And then he was naked in front of her.

It could have been scary. It could have been awkward. It was her first time. He was practically a stranger. A single word, a single look could have ruined the moment.

But instead, he reached out and brushed his fingers down the line of her cheek. Rested his fingertips against her mouth.

Then he said, an aching note in his voice, "This feels . . ."

"Like fate."

"Like heaven."

She smiled.

Then she reached down, opened her purse and pulled free protection. She'd grabbed the condom years ago at the student health center. She never thought she'd actually need it. Now, she was so thankful she'd kept it with her all that time.

"You said you're leaving in the morning?"

He nodded. Watched as she unwrapped the condom.

"Okay."

That meant they had the night.

Then they were on the bed. He was above her, and she was looking up at him, sinking into the mattress as he pressed her beneath him. She let out a long breath as his legs came over hers. She was smooth and soft, where he was rough and angled. Slowly, he lowered himself over her, so that every part of them touched. Skin to skin. Mouth to mouth.

When she was lying down she didn't have to strain to reach his mouth. She decided that lying on a bed was the perfect position for kissing. He stroked his hands over her hips. Tangled his fingers over her nipples and along the sides of her breasts. He kissed the underside of her jaw and trailed his mouth down her neck. She sought his mouth. Searched out the places that made him growl and hum.

The longer they kissed, the more his body caressed hers, the more her blood throbbed. Her skin became sensitized to every touch and whisper, until a breath sent her spiraling into a haze of need.

Until she rocked beneath him in a rhythm that he started, but she followed. She tilted toward him. Clung to him. Felt the sweat lining his back and the harshness of his exhales as he rocked against her. His finger sought her out, ran over her so that she cried out. There was a tightness, a need. She arched into his hand.

Then he settled at her entrance.

"Yes." She didn't know whether or not she said it out loud. So she said it again. "Yes."

There were tears at the corners of her eyes. She felt their heat. He kissed them.

Then he was pressing inside her. And she sobbed against his shoulder. It felt . . . He was right. It felt like heaven.

They came together, moving, and kissing, and seeking.

He whispered her name. Breathed it like a prayer.

She arched into him, the tightness, all the fire and pulsing, coursing need, constricted into a single desperate ball, and then he *moved*.

He thrust into her. Desperate. Needing. Until he was moving so hard, so fast, that she was swept up into him. He reached down, kissed his fingers over her. And with one stroke, a final kiss, she was clenching, crying, shattering.

She tightened around him, her body was outside her control as she gripped him. He grabbed her hands, thrust again, again. A desperate joining. And then she felt him. He came with a cry wrenched from him. He moved as he came, pouring himself into her.

She fell apart around him. He fell apart inside her. And they held each other together.

He slowed, until they finally stilled, legs and arms clasped tight. He was still inside her. Corey could feel her heart beating, pounding against him, his heart echoing in response.

He was shuddering, breathing hard as he kissed the edge of her lips.

She tasted the salt of tears. For a second she thought she'd been crying. It had felt so wonderful, so right, but then she realized they weren't her tears. They were his.

❧

New York, NY
    Lee

Lee had never thought that he'd see heaven, but lying in the dark, Corey tucked against him, he decided he'd been wrong. Heaven was right here.

She felt so good wrapped up in him and around him. There was a niggling of fear pressing at the edges of the euphoria, but he did his best to ignore it. After all, the morning was soon enough to castigate himself for making love with someone he'd only met twice in his entire life. That wasn't what the fear was about though.

As he pressed a kiss to the edge of her mouth, he tasted the salt of tears.

He couldn't quite comprehend that they were his. But they had to be. For the first time in his memory, tears leaked out of his eyes. He wasn't sad. He was the opposite. There wasn't any reason for them.

He'd just experienced something he never thought he would. He said it was heaven, but maybe heaven was just another word for love.

That was why there were those stray tears. They'd stopped now. But this feeling? Well. The only people who ever loved him—his family—somehow he was certain even now that his family had loved him . . . Jackson and Saul—the both of them—the only people he'd loved, he lost.

Sometimes he was scared that he was getting too close to Cordelia. But then he reminded himself that they'd never meet, he wouldn't love her, so he couldn't possibly lose her.

He liked her, he cared for her, he needed her, but he refused to love her. He couldn't let himself do that. That way she wouldn't ever leave him. He'd have her friendship, like the old lady in Romeo had claimed, for the rest of her life.

He knew it wasn't logical. He counted facts as among his closest friends. It didn't matter though, he still lived following that rule. Don't get too close to people. Be wary. Don't love freely.

Even with Jackson and Saul he'd kept back his words. Questioning whether or not he should let them know he cared.

So the tears, he knew, were the result of knowing that he'd tasted heaven only to lose it.

In a little more than five hours he was catching a taxi for JFK. He was leaving the country and he wouldn't be back for at least two years. Where he was going there wasn't postal service, or internet, there was a sat phone used once a month. So really, before anything could begin, it was already over.

So when Corey had said *I don't want to miss you.* Yes. He knew exactly what she meant. He already missed her.

She was warm. Her legs were tangled with his, and the smooth skin of her calves stroked along his legs. The white line of her naked shoulder glowed in the golden light that whispered through the window. He could feel the soft puff of her breath against his neck where her lips pressed a soft kiss. His heart lurched at the press of her mouth.

He was still inside her. He didn't want to leave the warmth of her. But she shifted beneath him, crumpling the white sheets that pooled beneath her. Before he left her, he pressed one last kiss to the corner of her mouth. She smelled like flowers. He'd noticed it right away. The last time they'd met she smelled like Christmas. But this time, she smelled like a wildflower meadow blooming in the sun. He could lie in her and breathe in her scent all day long.

"Am I crushing you?" He looked down at her, resting over her on his forearms.

"It's alright. I don't mind." She reached up and hesitantly brushed his hair back from his forehead.

She was so sweet. The smile in her eyes nearly broke him. He'd never imagined anyone like her wanting him, not in his whole life. He felt so grateful for her. How strange was that? To feel so grateful for the touch of another human being.

But he was crushing her. He was at least a foot taller and sixty pounds heavier than her. So even though he didn't want to, he pulled free. She inhaled sharply as he did. He rolled onto his back and stared at the ceiling, gray instead of white in the darkness.

Her voice was loud in the quiet hum of the room. "That was . . ."

He hummed in agreement.

"My whole body is tingling. I think I almost passed out," she admitted.

The corner of his mouth kicked up in a smile. He reached over and threaded his fingers through hers. He was warm, content, euphoric and buzzing. He ignored the anxiety biting at the edges of his euphoric cloud.

"I'm really glad I ran into you."

"Me too." He turned his head. The pillow shifted under him. He could see the outline of her cheeks, the waves of her dark auburn hair, inky in the dark, and the deep pools of her—hazel?—eyes. She turned on her side and rested her cheek on her hand.

"So. You're leaving in the morning?"

His throat tightened as if a hand clenched and squeezed, suffocating him. There was the anxiety. The fear.

He nodded.

She waited for him to say something. He couldn't.

"Well, I'm . . . I live in New York. Upstate actually. If you ever . . ." There must've been something in his expression. He didn't know what, but she trailed off. "You know. Never mind. I have a friend who told me 'live for the moment.' So live for . . . tonight. Right?"

There was a war raging inside him. One part denied what she said, howled at it and kicked and hit. It didn't want just tonight. It wanted all the nights. Another part, though, fought back. It agreed with her. If tonight was all there was, then he'd never really had heaven after all. It was lost before he'd arrived. But losing heaven tonight was better than losing it after he grew used to it. Quick pain is always better than a long fester.

Besides he was leaving. For years. He had nothing to give. No promises. No words.

He just had a night.

A moment.

She waited in the silence, her gaze dropping. Then she let out a shuddering exhale.

He reached out and pressed his fingers to the soft skin of her collarbone. Curled his hand there. He could feel the reverberation of her heart. It wasn't a frantic hard beat anymore. Now, it was soft and slow. A quiet vibration.

"Thank you."

Her eyes widened, and her hair fell across her face as she tilted toward him. "For what?"

He thought about the woods. The quiet there. The snow coating the balsam fir and muffling the sounds. He thought about all the things left unspoken.

"For wanting to see me again. For giving me the best night of my entire life. For . . . just . . . for being you. I've never known anyone like you before."

She smiled at that and it was the smile he remembered. The one from two years ago that had stunned him, confused him, and made him resentful. He wasn't resentful this time because he knew, it really was for him.

Suddenly, he wanted a chocolate cake. Hot cocoa. Peppermint. He wanted to stay up all night with her and eat chocolate cake with their hands and talk. Maybe she'd talk so much that her words would fill up an entire year. He'd like that.

In the months to come he'd bring out their conversations and relive them. He knew the job he'd taken was dangerous. He was running medical supplies for an international aid organization to remote areas in conflict zones and war-torn areas. He'd start in Iraq and then move to wherever he was needed. He'd signed on for two years to start. Maybe he'd stay with the job longer.

But during the long drives across rough, remote terrain, wouldn't it be nice to remember a night of chocolate cake and laughter?

"I'm not coming back to New York anytime soon," he said, and even though it was dark, he thought he caught the dampening of her expression. "But . . ." he wrinkled his brow, "would you like a piece of chocolate cake? A hot cocoa? There's a shop down the street that's open until midnight. I could run over and grab some and we could . . . we'd have the night."

It was the least eloquent thing he'd ever said. This was one of those times when he wished he could talk like he wrote. He could always write everything that he wanted to say.

She lifted onto her elbow, and the white comforter fell around her like a snowbank shining in moonlight. The room was warm, and her floral scent spilled around him.

He smiled at her hopefully.

Maybe when he came back after years away they'd run into each other again. Maybe they could plan for it. He'd ask her. Two years from now. At the skating rink at Rockefeller. No, not there. At Old Freddy's tree stand on

Third Avenue or maybe at the Christmas Market in Union Square.

Maybe in two years whatever this was between them would be gone. Burned out and blown away like ashes on the wind. Or maybe it would be just the same or stronger still. He wanted to find out.

"Alright." She smiled at him. Sat up and tucked the blanket around her lap. Her eyes were large pools, and he nearly fell into them again. "I love chocolate cake. And hot cocoa. Or coffee, so I can stay up all night."

At her smile, a happy ribbon wound through his heart. It tightened in a loop and squeezed.

Relief coursed through him, and he let out a long breath. He didn't know why it was essential that she stayed the night. He only knew it was.

The heater hummed in the corner, letting out warm, dry air and a soft, pleasant whir. The hotel room, small before, now seemed expansive and wide open with a million possibilities. The quiet was pregnant with expectancy.

"Coffee," he agreed. "Cake, coffee, the night. I'll be right back. Don't go anywhere."

He said the last with a smile.

Then she surprised him by leaning forward and pressing a hard kiss to his mouth. Her lips were warm and soft. She tasted like flowers peeking up through the snow. A rush of blood worked its way down from his head. She gripped his shoulders and kissed him again and again.

He almost pushed her down to the bed again. Forget the cake and coffee, they'd stay in bed all night. But then he remembered how she licked frosting from her fingers.

And he remembered how funny she was when she got to talking.

So when her lips left his, he gave her one last hard kiss and said, "Don't move. I'll be back."

He took a thirty-second shower. Got dressed. Hurried out of the hotel. Down the block. Bought three pieces of chocolate cake—just because. Two coffees—enough creamer and sugar for an army. A hot cocoa—just in case. A bouquet of red roses wrapped in glossy brown paper— because he thought she might like them. Then he hurried back to the room, opened the door.

"I got enough cake for . . ."

He trailed off.

The lights were still off. It didn't matter. He could see well enough.

The room was empty.

She was gone.

Corey hurried down the sidewalk, the heels of her boots clicking on the pavement. She tugged her coat close and buried her chin in her scarf. She kept her eyes on the gray concrete and refused to look up or back. The icy wind pulled at her, but she ignored it.

She wanted to go back.

Chris might not have returned from the shop yet. He wouldn't even know she'd left. She could run through the lobby, ride the elevator, and throw herself back into bed.

And then?

Well. Then they'd have cake and coffee. And probably make love again. It would be . . . heartbreaking. It would break her heart.

Corey wondered what Lee would say about all this. He probably would tell her to stop complaining and face the facts. Chris was leaving. He wasn't coming back. He wasn't interested in anything beyond tonight. Even if he did say it was the best night of his life. Heaven.

Maybe Lee would tell her she was living in denial. She was *actually* leaving because she didn't want to be hurt. He'd tell her to say the truth. The truth was, she'd thought it was fate. She'd thought maybe it was even love (a new shoot of love, like the green sprout rising up from a spring bulb, fragile and precious). While he thought . . . he thought they wouldn't see each other again after tonight.

Well, Corey knew something from her two decades of life. Just like plants, love can't grow without sunshine, it can't survive without water, love has to be fed.

So she snipped the little shoot off before it could wither and die.

She left.

"I shouldn't have left." The husky croak of her voice startled a couple walking past. They shot her a suspicious look and crossed the street to the other sidewalk.

Corey sighed and tugged her coat close when the icy wind grabbed her. She turned west, back toward Chelsea and the hotel room she shared with Elizabeth. It was late. Nearly midnight. The streets were quiet and dark, lit only by the silvery glow of streetlamps and the reflection of red and green streetlights off the glass of apartment buildings and high rises. There was the sound of wind curving around buildings, the soft hiss of passing taxis, and the occasional footsteps of other pedestrians. But beyond that, the night was just what it seemed, quiet and dark.

Ahead, The Highline no longer looked like a magical cloud garden. It was a dark form hunched in solitude over the streets.

"I shouldn't have left. No. I should have left." She went back and forth with herself like she was plucking petals from a daisy. He loves me, he loves me not.

Then, because she was practical, and had already survived more in twenty years than most, *and* because she always laughed at herself, she smiled up at the starless night.

It was just one night in a long life.

It was just one man who she'd never see again.

It was just a quick dream that had already ended.

She wouldn't feel sorry for herself.

She wouldn't regret it.

She wouldn't ask for more than he wanted to give.

Wasn't that what she'd always told herself? If she ever loved she wouldn't expect anything in return. He said that she'd given him the best night of his life.

Well, he gave her the same.

It was the best night. But even the best things had to end.

She was glad she'd met him again. She was glad they'd made love. She was *glad*.

She wouldn't regret him. She wouldn't be upset with him for not being able to give more. She'd just . . . keep going. She'd keep ticking, like a heart who only knew how to push one beat after another.

She had classes and an internship to finish. A Hobday Christmas to celebrate. A flower shop to open.

And . . . she smiled across the darkened street at the welcoming golden lights of her hotel . . . soon, she'd have a Christmas card to write.

five years and nine months ago

9

———————

FIVE YEARS AND NINE MONTHS AGO

Cordelia Hobday
   1621 Tenderfoot Lane
   Romeo, NY

Dear Cordelia,

Did you get my Christmas card? The birthday letter I sent? I don't think you did. Although, maybe you have, and your replies haven't reached me yet. I guess there's no way to know. Cruise, he's my superior, says that sending a letter from here is like tossing a piece of paper into the wind and hoping it arrives back in America. My letters are as likely to reach you as if I stuck them to a wish and a prayer.

But maybe this one . . . I'll keep writing until I hear from you. The return address is where you can send letters, it's outside London, at the head office and they'll know where I am and how to send it on, usually by handing it to another aid worker coming my way. They told me that sometimes it's like a chain of hand-offs, letters working their way deeper into the field, in places where the post doesn't go. Sometimes they'll hold letters in London since I'm supposed to go up for training twice a year. Sometimes they'll send them to a depot where we go to pick up supplies.

But if everything is working properly it takes about two to three months for the mail to get through. Don't send brownies unless you want to feed someone besides me. They'll be devoured long before they reach me. That's a joke. Sort of. Maybe it's the only one that I'll be able to tell in this letter.

Because, Cordelia, it hurts here. That's what I've been meaning to say. It hurts. I don't mean the land, it's a deeper pain than that. In Iraq, the earth was covered in sloping sand dunes, salt-covered and dry. The sun burned my eyes and I found myself coveting every sliver of shade. But it wasn't that. No. I mean, it *hurts*.

I used to feel alone. I used to wish for a break in the quiet. Now I don't have time or energy to feel. I started in London. A month of training and orientation. And then I flew into southern Iraq, into the dunes where ancient mud brick ruins and ziggurats rose from the sand. I was stunned by the realization that thousands of years ago, people built a great civilization here. They had the same desires as us. To live, to maybe love, to find a purpose or perhaps just to struggle to survive. They were like us. And then their lives washed away and their memory was buried in the sand.

Now what's left?

Some ziggurats are destroyed. Bombed. Bulldozed. Burned. Acid churned in my stomach when I saw that. How could we be so careless to destroy a monument thousands of years old? Those bricks had stood through all the history we know, Mesopotamia, the Greeks, the Romans, the Middle Ages. Julius Caesar. Joan of Arc. Shakespeare. It survived eons. We're like thoughtless children with toy airplanes rampaging the earth. It wasn't one person who dropped a bomb and destroyed our history. It was all of us.

At least that's how it feels. I drove medical supplies to a village deep in a conflict zone. There were people there who hadn't had medical treatment in years. Small things that without medicine had become large things. Growing up like I did, I never took medical care for granted. But I was always healthy. Quick on my feet. I never realized how lucky I was. Yes, even me. I had pharmacies, over the counter medicine, toothbrushes and toothpaste, walk-in free clinics.

We spent two months in Iraq. I'm in South Sudan now. Did I tell you I'd be moving around so much? The organization I'm working for sends medical supplies into the worst conflict zones, where even seasoned military veterans don't want to tread.

Do you remember how we promised to always tell the truth? Here's the truth. I'm scared. The fear twists in my stomach and keeps me awake at night. It's a catastrophe here. I don't understand why there is darkness in this world. I don't understand the pain that permeates the landscape here like a fog clinging and smothering the earth. I want to leave. Every day I wake up and want to leave.

But then I remember the faces of the people I've helped. The little boy who raced to me, his face shining because I had an antibiotic for his grandmother. The young father who shook my hands in thanks when I gave him the anti-parasitic for his young son. The man who took me into his one room home and fed me a dinner of bread and tea in gratitude for the topical anesthetic and sutures that let him stitch up his brother after he was attacked.

If the darkness is a fog, then let me be the light. That's what I pray every morning when I wake up afraid. Let me be the sun that clears it away. I know I'm not enough to clear it all. But maybe I'm enough for one person, and then another, and another. Do you think? I don't know. I'm overwhelmed most days. I can't, no, don't want to describe it to you. The horrors we put on ourselves. I wasn't expecting this. I hadn't imagined it. I only . . . I'd wanted to find my way home.

But I think I've gone off course. Yet I can't leave. Now that I'm here. I can't leave. I need to stay, no matter how afraid I am. We'll go to Chad next. Soon, I think.

Write me. Tell me about flowers. About your Christmas. Tell me about the good in the world. I don't see much of it anymore. I'm trying to be the good here. I told you I'd be careful, that I was always alright. I guess that wasn't true. I'm not alright. Even if I'm careful, it might not be enough.

I keep thinking about you. About the candlelight in your windows at Christmas and the snow coating your front porch. The scent of lemon zest in sugar cookies and your chocolate chip brownies. Did you know, I met someone last year, I thought it felt like love, but looking back on it, I can't remember exactly what she looked like, or what she felt like, and the harder I try, the more I forget. It's funny because when I think of her, my mind goes blank, and then all I can think of is you. Your stories, your humor, your holding my hand through your letters.

I could really use your hand right now.

I'm writing this letter by the light of the full moon. The yellow glow shines off the night black leaves and illuminates the pages. It's March now, the beginning of the rainy season. During the day the sun heats the earth to a hundred scorching degrees. After the sun sets, the heat recedes to merely unbearably hot instead of deathly hot. I guess that's the winter-lover in me speaking. The air here has a thick, humid, astringent smell that sticks in my throat and burns my eyes. Right now, the bugs are feasting on me, but if I go inside there won't be any light to write by. Electricity is a rare commodity.

Maybe someday I'll call you. Or send an email. Even if it is against our rules. Wouldn't that be funny? But computers and phones are much scarcer than paper. I have my notebook and a dozen envelopes. And besides, what would I say over the phone? Like you said, there's something about the lead of a pencil that arrows straight to a heart and lets you write exactly what you mean to say. I worry that over the phone the only thing you'd hear is silence and the crackle of the line.

So never mind on the phone call or email. Just write me. I hope this letter finds you. If not, I'll try again.

I'm glad I have you. I feel better. Maybe I won't find home by coming here. I know I won't. But I have found another reason for being here. I have to help. Like Cruise says, if you stick around for the first three months, then you'll stick around for the two years. It was three months yesterday. I'm still here. He used to always say, "Night, Weston. I'll bet you leave tomorrow." But last night, he just said, "Night, Weston." For some reason that felt like the biggest accomplishment.

By the way, I'm waiting to hear about For the Love of Flowers. Will it be in Romeo near where the Christmas Market was? Will you have a signature flower? Has your genius at arranging been recognized yet? Are you still hauling manure water or are you now running the shop single-handedly?

By the way, there's a bushy, thick plant here with cardinal red flowers. Do you know what it is? Cruise doesn't know anything about flowers and only grunted when I asked him. But it makes me think of you. It has petals that are as soft as a rose. I thought you'd like it. I'm including a drawing. Maybe you'll recognize it. I guess it reminds me, there's beauty everywhere, you just have to look around. I know we're driving into the worst places, purposely seeking the dark, I know my view is distorted, and if I only drove a little farther then I'd find the sun peeking over the horizon. There is good everywhere, isn't there? Do you think?

I'm looking up at the sky. The stars are pinprick bright and I don't recognize any of them. The North Star is nowhere to be seen. I guess it's really true that we don't share the same sky anymore. The constellations are different here. But the moon is the same.

I miss you. I miss your straight, blocky letters. How you loop your s and slash your t. I miss how your o never quite connects at the top, like you're leaving room for something to fill the inside of it up. Write me. Even if, like you said before, it's only in your heart and never makes it across the world.

Write me.

—Lee

~

Five years and eight months ago

Lee Weston
c/o I.A.O. West
514 Hannocks Crossing #2
Luton, Bedfordshire
U.K.

Dear Lee,

I have to write that again. Lee. Thank *God*. Thank God. I've been so worried. You told me not to worry, but how couldn't I? Christmas came and went, and there was no letter. New Year's, January, February, March—no letter. Do you remember that first year when I told you that I imagined you either a multimillionaire with a kangaroo or sliced up by the Dorito killer? Those imaginings were *nothing*. For the past months, I imagined worse.

A world without you.

Never knowing what happened. Where you went.

How you left. A lifetime of Christmases when you weren't there.

I'm holding your letter. It's worse for wear. It arrived crumpled, stained with unidentifiable streaks of black and gray, the edges ripped and curled from water damage. Yet it *arrived*.

Every day since December fifteenth, I'd been holding my breath when I pulled open the mailbox. And then as the days passed, my worry grew. I've been lying awake nights staring at the ceiling, praying you were okay.

I have to admit, when I saw your handwriting on the envelope, I cried. I burst into big, hiccupping sobs. All that fear for you was bound up inside me in this giant churning lake. And when I saw your letter, all of it gushed out of me in messy, noisy tears.

My mom thought something had happened. She shouted, "David (that's my dad) call the ambulance!"

She's a worrier, remember? Lately, it's been a million times worse.

But I waved her off and ran upstairs to read your letter again and again. I read it enough times to reassure myself that you were alive. Still here.

You once said that no one would notice if you'd gone, no one would care if you died. Lee, I care. I care. Those words don't even describe . . . they can't.

In mid-January when the worry was eating at me I walked to church. It was a Monday morning, and cold outside. I walked down the aisle. The church was empty and hushed, morning Mass had already finished. On Christmas I'd lit a candle for you during my family's candle-lighting tradition. But that Monday, I lit another.

I stood at the front of the church, touched a flame to

the wick, and prayed that you were okay. The candle burned all day until the flame went out.

And then I went back the next morning. And the next. I lit a candle for you every day.

You said you can't see the North Star anymore. Maybe the candles I'm lighting can be your North Star. Maybe they can be what guides you home.

Didn't the ancient sailors use the North Star to navigate the unknown seas? When the black waters and the dark skies were a vast, empty, chaotic unknown, didn't they point their bows to the North Star?

If you can't see it anymore, let the candles I light be your star. I'll keep them burning until I know you're safely home.

I don't know if or when this letter will reach you. I'm not quite sure I agree about not calling or emailing. Even the quiet crackle of a phone line is better than the silence of not knowing. But, oh, it's so hard to write what I'm feeling. The *relief.*

I hugged your letter to my chest. I want to hug you. Pretend that I am. You asked me to tell you about something good. Right now, it's early spring. The sky is robin's egg blue, and during the day the sun is a gentle warmth. The sounds of snow melting are everywhere in the *drip, drip* of icicles melting, to the gurgle of snowbanks melting in little rivulets that run in temporary rivers down the streets. There's a tinkle and pop and crack as snow melts in the sun. Do you remember that sound?

And the smell of spring. The sharp, cold scent of melting ice and snow. The muddy, grassy smell of the ground waking up. Even the small green leaves unfurling from the trees have a smell.

At Mrs. Krantz's shop I'm surrounded by all the spring flowers—bright yellow daffodils, white narcissus, and bubblegum colored hyacinth, and tulips. Lee, we have tulips in every color ever found on earth. I'm covered in pollen at the end of the day. Dusted like a fairy in yellow and white and pink. It's on my hands, my cheeks, my nose. I smell like Easter. Candy sweet and softly floral. If you could see me, you'd laugh.

Yesterday, I saw a robin poking at a bright green patch of grass, the only melted spot in the shop's front yard. I had an armful of long-stemmed tulips and a planter of hyacinth I was delivering. But I was so distracted, so delighted by the robin, that I slipped on a mud puddle that had frozen over.

Don't worry. I landed on my butt. The thin sheet of ice cracked and I sank into three inches of cold, wet, muddy goo. My pants, my boots, the back of my jacket were all covered in brown icy mud.

But here's the best part. I saved the flowers. Not a single petal fell off the tulips. Not one hyacinth was knocked askew. As my feet slipped out from under me and I flipped backward, I held those pots high over my head, like I was holding up the Olympic torch. The rest of the day, I wore my mud like a badge of honor.

To answer your question, no I'm not running the shop yet. But soon I'll be finished with classes and my internship and then … then …

I told you that I'd open For the Love of Flowers. But plans change, don't they?

I wrote you. Back when I first found out. I didn't know who else to tell.

I suppose I needed to tell you first because you wouldn't worry like my family. You wouldn't judge me.

And you wouldn't tell me what to do or think. I'd just needed to write it down and send it off.

So anyway, I wrote you.

I sent my letter to New Brunswick, but it came back to me. I suppose you aren't receiving mail there anymore. But it was okay. After I wrote you, I wasn't so scared anymore. I wasn't so confused.

By the time your letter came back I already knew what to do.

So anyway, the season isn't the only thing changing in Romeo.

I'm pregnant, Lee.

Actually, I think, by the time you receive my letter, or by the time you get my next letter, I'll be a mom.

That's a strange thing to write. I'll be a mom.

I have so many feelings about it—some of them big, some of them small. Before you wonder, no, I didn't get married. I'm not in a relationship. The dad isn't around. It's just me and the baby. Well, and my parents, my siblings, and my nine hundred relatives. There won't be a shortage of love. This kid is going to grow up in the noisiest, busiest, most affectionate family on the planet. God help them.

You asked me to tell you something good. I'll admit, I'm scared. I didn't plan for this, and I didn't expect it. I didn't really believe it for at least the first two weeks. Then I started gagging whenever I smelled the manure juice at work, and then boy, did I believe it.

But here's what's good. I'm scared. I'm wondering how I'm going to make this work. I'm worried about my family worrying about me. But then, just last week, I was at work, stripping thorns off a shipment of roses when I felt it. A little butterfly kiss of a flutter. It felt just like a butterfly tickling me from the inside. I pressed my hand to my belly and I felt it again. I stood there, I don't know how long. Something inside me just cracked open and I felt so happy.

Before that, it hadn't felt real. I didn't feel connected at all. But then, she or he kicked or somersaulted or waved. I whispered back, "Hello." And they gave that butterfly kiss again.

Maybe that's not what you were asking for. But it felt . . . it felt like a ray of sunshine warming the ground in spring. I wish you could feel it too, that new life. That hope.

My family is scared for me. They don't understand how I could've gotten pregnant (well, beyond the mechanics, that part is obvious). They don't understand why the dad isn't in the picture. They worry about how dangerous it is for me to even have a baby. Because that's the thing. Pregnancy is hard on your cardiovascular system.

Your blood volume increases 45%, your cardiac output increases, your heart rate speeds up. It's a strain.

Lee, you always face the facts. I'm facing them too. I know it's a strain.

But I'm counting on modern medicine. I'm putting faith in the high-risk doctors and their careful monitoring. I'm . . .

My mom, when I first told her, she cried. I haven't seen her cry in years. Then she said, face pale and scared, "No one will blame you if you don't carry this baby."

And for a minute—more—I thought about it.

"You could die," she whispered.

But that didn't worry me because people have been telling me I could die since I was four years old.

Then she said, "Cordelia. This baby won't ever love you as much as I do. I don't want you to risk your life. Not for them."

And I suppose her saying that—my mom—was what cemented what I'd already been feeling. This baby might not love me as much as my mom does, maybe they never will, but I'll love my baby as much as my mom loves me. And so, after that, there wasn't a question any more.

Yes, it's dangerous. Yes, there's no father. Yes, I'm young, some might say, too young. Sure, I haven't gotten a loan for my shop, and I'll have to use my savings for my baby instead of my business. I know all this. I'm okay with it.

But can I tell you something?

The dad, I felt about him the way I feel about you. He was one of the best things that ever happened to me. I don't regret him. I won't. It's not often you meet someone that you connect with on such a deep level. There was him. And there's you. That's it. Two people in my whole life.

Maybe you understand what I'm trying to say. Or maybe you don't. I'm not sure how you feel about babies. But hey, your best friend by letter is having one, so he (or she) is in your life now. For good. Next time I write, my letter will probably be filled with news all about him (her?).

Don't worry. I'll be alright. I know I'm using your line. But I will. I'll come out safe. My family will smother me in worry and love.

I have a job lined up at the local grocer in their florist area. Maybe in five years or so I'll have saved enough to start my own place. Elizabeth understands. She's going to stay on with Mrs. Krantz for a while longer. She's even offered to babysit the "little monster." Although, if there's one thing I'm not short of, it's babysitters.

I don't know. I'm sorry. Your letter finally reached me and here I am telling you my own concerns. They're not too big. I'll be alright. My heart is strong, I'm sure. I still have the wooden heart ornament you made me hanging from my bed post, just in case I need a little extra help.

I think of you every day. I'll write you letters in my heart every single day and send them along when I light your candle.

I wish you were here. Right now. With me. I'll describe the moment for you so that when you look back on this night, you might remember it and realize we were under the same moon.

I'm sitting in my bedroom with my own ugly paisley wallpaper and white cotton curtains. My window is open, and I can smell the night spring smells—snow, wet bark, new grass. The sky has just slipped to indigo, and the newly arrived whip-poor-will by my window is letting out his final whip-poor-will trill. The curtain brushes against the windowsill in the cool night breeze, making a soft whispering noise.

I'm sitting cross-legged on my bed, and the old mattress sinks beneath me. I have my notebook resting on my belly and my pen scratches over the paper. The baby is moving, knocking around. Dusk is his (her?) favorite time to flutter. I'm tired, sleepy and sore and hungry. I might sneak down and have a snack before bed.

But before that, it's March 23, there's the moon, silver and nearly full. There's just a small smudge of darkness at its edge.

Do you remember this moon? It's glowing through my window, illuminating the old, wavy glass.

Here, it's a peaceful, quiet, hopeful moon. I'm holding out my hand for you. You can thread your fingers through mine. You can settle on my twin bed next to me. We'll crowd in together and share a pillow. You can rest your head on my shoulder. I'll put my arms around you. We'll listen to the whip-poor-will until he falls quiet and the world goes to sleep.

Don't worry about being scared. Sometimes I'm scared too. In fact, there were times in my life when the fear was so big that it was like a monster living inside me. Somedays it devoured me and tore into me.

When I was young I would hide so my family couldn't see or hear, and I would cry I was so afraid. But Lee. We weren't made to be afraid. I don't think God made us to be afraid.

So here's what I did. Maybe it's what you can do too. Hug the fear. Love it. Open your arms, and invite it inside, and let it consume you. And once it has eaten every part of you and paralyzed you and ravaged you. Well, it's done its worst. Thank it. And then, I promise, it will walk away and leave you with room for other feelings.

Like happiness. And peace. And compassion. I don't think we were made to always live in fear.

Everyone is so afraid that I'll die. But there are so many worse things that can happen to a person than death. Most of them we do to ourselves.

I can't tell you not to be afraid. I can only tell you that there are bigger things, more powerful things than fear.

You already have them. I know.

I've always believed there is no fear in love.

Lee, there is no fear in love.

I'm holding your hand. Sending you love.

Please be careful. Keep on. Do what you feel you have

to. Bring good to others. Be a warm light of hope. I can't tell you to be anything less. I won't. But I'll keep lighting a candle for you. I'll keep holding my breath when I check the mailbox.

Write me before Christmas. Write me and tell me you're okay. Write and suggest a name for my baby. Write me and tell me that you don't think I'm making a mistake or tell me that you think I am. I don't care as long as you write.

Yours,
Cordelia

P.S. Also, I forgot, the flower you drew is the hibiscus. Don't give it to anyone unless you really like them as it represents deep romantic love and passion. If you dry the flowers you can drink it as a tea. It's tart and sweet, like me. Be safe, Lee.

five years and five months ago

10

———————

FIVE YEARS AND FIVE MONTHS AGO

Cordelia Hobday
   1621 Tenderfoot Lane
   Romeo, NY

Dear Cordelia,

A mom? You're a mom? Cordelia. You're a mom. You have to be by now. I didn't receive your letter until summer, it trailed after me through Chad, Libya, and found me in a small, remote village at the edge of Bwindi Impenetrable.

You should've seen me when Niev handed me your letter, it was like I'd been lit on fire. He'd been dispatched from Kampala. Yesterday, he received a shipment of polio vaccines, your letter in tow. Cruise knew exactly what it was. He'd seen me writing you in the dark too many nights not to realize. I raced to the truck, slammed the door shut, and suffered the suffocating heat so that I could have a moment of quiet to *read*. My hands shook as I ripped open your envelope. They're still shaking.

It's so good to hear from you. To hear your voice reaching through your letter. That doesn't even make sense. I've never heard you speak, but I can still hear your words.

You asked me not to worry about you. I guess, my worry would be wasted, you're either okay or you're not. It's done already, isn't it? You're a mom.

Of all the things I imagined happening with you, that wasn't one of them. I can't tell you that you made the right choice or the wrong choice. What do I know about choices? I only know that here, last month, I saw a woman who had walked three days to deliver her baby at the nearest hospital. She'd started bleeding four days before. Neither the mom or the baby survived.

That's not the sort of thing you need to hear. I'm sorry. I've lost any of the social niceties I once had. I've been stripped down, weathered by the rough, abrasive sand of the deserts and the humid, oppressive heat of the tropical forests. I'm not really fit for people anymore. But what I was trying to say was, a lot of people here don't have a choice. I see it every day. The only choice they have is whether to give in to anger or despair or to keep going through it all, sharing a bit of kindness along the way. That's the only choice I know about. I won't tell you not to risk your life. I won't say whether that's right or wrong.

I am selfish, though. You're mine. I claimed you years ago, and I want you to be okay. If I could talk to the father of your baby, I'd tell him to show more care. He was careless with someone I . . . you're invaluable. You are . . . you wrote about lighting me a candle every day, but Cordelia, it isn't the candle, it's you who's my bright flame. If you went out, where would that leave me?

I guess it's too late to suggest a name. But if I had a baby, I'd name them Gabriel. Boy or girl, it doesn't matter. I don't know why, but I've always liked that name. Maybe it's because someone in my family was named Gabriel. I don't know. I don't actually remember anything before I was six years old. The social workers from foster care said it was trauma induced amnesia. The brain does whatever it can to protect itself, so whatever happened, I guess it was too much for me, so my brain formed a memory shell, like a walnut shell around a soft core. It's impenetrable. Sometimes I'll catch flickers, like my false Christmas memory. Other times I'll have slivers of pictures in dreams. I wonder if I ever do meet my family, if they'll be disappointed that I don't know them. That I don't have any memories of them. I'm not sure. But, Gabriel. That's a name I'd suggest.

I'm trying to picture you as a mom. It's hard. We've been writing so long, since we were practically kids, and I guess I never thought about the fact that someday *we* might have kids, or get married, or fall in love, or end up across the world from each other.

I agree. Things change. Plans change.

I want you to promise me something. Take care of yourself. I know you have your family. I know you have your friends. But I'm not sure they'll know what you need. I think you have a habit of hiding yourself from them. So I'm going to tell you what to do and you have to listen to me because I'm your friend and I care.

First, when you're tired, don't push through, don't

brush it off. Sit down on your old couch in front of the fire, pull a blanket on your lap and read one of the books you love so much.

Second, if you feel like you need to cry, put on a movie with sad music, sad scenes, and let yourself cry. No one will mind and no one will know that you've been waiting to cry for a long, long time. If you want you can imagine that I'm there holding you.

Third, eat as many lemon sugar cookies as you like, but also make sure to eat good things too, like chicken soup or the garlic mashed potatoes with melted butter that you love.

Fourth, you make other people flowers, but save some for yourself. A bouquet of roses and hibiscus or a small bunch of violets. You deserve flowers too.

Fifth, when the baby comes, you can give them all your love, but be sure to save some of that love for yourself. Live. I've seen too much here. I know that your mom's right, life is so easily extinguished. Please live. If you're teetering on the edge, tilting one way then the other, and you need a final push, live for me.

When you wrote, *it's a strain*, I heard what you didn't say.

Death is a possibility.

I think, I never wanted to acknowledge this before, but there's something that I need to say. A truth. I'm afraid that you mean too much to me. If I care about someone as much as I care about you, then what would happen to me if you were gone?

We're friends. I think I don't deserve a friend like you. Someday I think you might have to help me become human again. After all this.

I'm glad you wrote to me about Romeo. About the

snow melting and the spring grass peeking up from the frozen ground. I don't remember the night you wrote about, it was too long ago. But I do know that I look at the moon, and wonder if you're watching it too. It's good to know that there's a place in the world that's peaceful, full of kindness and warmth. I think your home is a lot like you, a comfortable, warm place that has room for as many people as need it, a place with unlimited kindness. A great capacity for love.

That's how I know you'll be a good mom. Don't worry about being young, you're older than me. Don't worry about being on your own, you have me, at least by letter. And you have your family. Don't worry about money, or about not having enough to start your shop.

Did I tell you? Jackson and Saul left me the cabin and the land. I sold it before I left, and because the amount made me nervous, it's more than I'll be able to spend in a lifetime, I left it in an account to gather interest. It turns out thousands of acres, a lifetime of saving and never spending meant that Jackson and Saul were wealthy. I don't need it. Next time I'm in London, I'm sending you enough to start For the Love of Flowers and enough to keep you and the baby alright for a long time.

There isn't any point in arguing. In fact, you may see the money before you see this letter, if you ever even get this letter. I want to do it, so don't say no. Please. You can pay me back if you like. You can even add interest. It's up to you. I have to do it, though, because I need to know that across the ocean, back in Romeo, you're there, surrounded by flowers, happy, doing what you always wanted, giving people joy.

I promise not to be like your uncle Hobday, bringing it up for the next twenty years. I just . . . I just want to know that there's still light out there, and you're my best chance at seeing that. I picture you with your flowers. I imagine you with your baby (girl? Boy?). I need to know that you're alive and happy. That's my selfish request. Please be alive. Please be happy. Please take care of yourself and accept this gift.

Someday I'm going to get up the courage to call you. If you answer, I might take a few seconds to reply, it'll be that good to hear your voice.

Do you think it's possible to care about someone so much that it feels like you've swallowed the moon? That description doesn't make sense. But here I am, still sitting in the truck, scribbling this letter back to you so that Niev can return with it to Kampala.

The tropical leaves of the forest are thick and black in the fading light and the vines that cover the understory are glistening silver in the moonlight. It's never looked so beautiful here.

The mahogany hills rising in the dusk, the riot of birds whistling and screeching, the mist rising through the tall grass, and the soft half glow of silvery gold that coats the land. Niev and Cruise walk the hill in the distance, their figures black shadows against the trees. A group of children run past them, shouting and laughing as they kick a ball in their final game before they're called to bed. The air smells of resin, loam, and mahogany, an earthy, spicy scent that's slightly sweet and heavier at dusk. And over it all, the moon shines, a full globe in the gray blue sky. It's painting us all in silver light and I feel . . .I feel as if all the glow has somehow ended up inside of me.

You're okay. I have to believe this. You're a mom. I don't know how, but you're right, I've already made room for your baby in my heart. It's carved, right there, in the center. It's because she's yours, I think.

Be okay, Cordelia.

I've kept my promise. I'm staying safe. Now, I'm asking you for yours. Be okay. Take care of yourself.

If this letter doesn't reach you for months, I'll say it now—

Merry Christmas, Cordelia.

Merry Christmas to you. Merry Christmas to your baby.

—Lee

P.S. I'm sending a wooden ornament I made. I wrote on the back, *First Christmas*. I hope that's okay. If you can't tell, it's a heart. If yours is alright you can give this one to the baby.

Five years and three months ago

Lee Weston
    c/o I.A.O. West
    514 Hannocks Crossing #2
    Luton, Bedfordshire
    U.K

Dear Lee,

I miss you. Can you miss someone you've never met? You must be able to because missing you is a constant in my life, as constant as the winter wind and the hollow night skies. Your letter reached me just in time. I wasn't quite a mom yet.

If I can tell the truth, which I always do with you, your letter helped me through. I think there must've been a postal angel watching over me. Making sure your words reached me.

Before I tell you more—Merry Christmas, Lee.

I think, by the time you read this, it will be Christmastime. I hope, wherever you are, you take a moment to make a Christmas wish.

Even if there aren't star-topped evergreens, cold-pinched cheeks, or skating in the snow, I hope that you make a wish.

My wish for you? That you stay safe. That you do whatever you have to. That even if you're stripped of everything else you keep your integrity. Your hope. Your kindness. Even if you can't see it in yourself, I see it in you.

I know you're worried that you'll come back changed, unfit to be around people anymore. You said you fear I'll have to help you become human again.

Lee, there is so much goodness in you. If you need me to be the mirror that helps you see that, I'll gladly do that for you. I'll be your mirror and you'll be my friend.

I still light a candle for you. Every day.

Do you still have my lucky penny? I wonder if it keeps you safe.

I want to tell you thank you. The money you sent arrived before your letter. I wouldn't have known what to think except the memo said, "*For the baby and For the Love of Flowers. Lee.*"

How could you send something like that and only sign it: *Lee.*

How could you send enough to build my dreams and make all the fear about raising my daughter (she's a girl, Lee) just evaporate?

How could you do that?

It made me want to hug you and shake you all at the same time. Laugh and cry all at once. Instead, I sat there at the kitchen table, staring at the couriered bank check, a stupid look on my face for at least thirty minutes.

Do you think it's funny that five years ago you wrote me a letter for ten dollars. And now? Look at us. I'm not sure you got a fair deal.

But Lee. Thank you.

I don't know how to say it, but thank you.

I'll make For the Love of Flowers an oasis. I'll make it an Eden of flowers, a peaceful, fragrant meadow. So that someday, if you come to Romeo, you can sit among the lilies and the roses and the begonias, and just . . . heal.

You won't have to speak. I won't mind the silence. We'll let the flowers do all the work.

Purple hyacinth for sorrow and healing. Roses for friendship and love. Snowdrop narcissus for new beginnings.

You can just sit and breathe in their floral perfume and they'll say everything that needs to be said. I'll make a haven for you and fill it with flowers.

Wherever you are, you can know it's always there for you.

I finished school. I finished my internship. I'm a mom. A mom, Lee.

You were right. I needed that push to live.

The day I got your letter I was at Mrs. Krantz's shop, hauling an order of long-stemmed roses from the delivery van to the storage room. They were all deep red, reserved for a wedding. There were hundreds of them gathered in heavy, water-filled buckets. Their odor filled the air, drenching me in its thick, floral scent. I was sweating, out of breath, arms shaking and heart pounding.

I was thirty-seven weeks pregnant. One minute I was lugging four dozen roses across the storage room, and the next...

I don't know.

My heart, it sputtered, hiccupped in my chest, and then—

That's all.

Elizabeth told me it was the scariest moment of her entire life. One second I was red-faced and laughing about how sweaty and out of breath I was and the next... I was flat on the floor, surrounded by forty-eight blood-red roses, their petals crushed beneath me, the cold water seeping into my clothes and spilling across the concrete.

I don't remember anything. It was quick the second between consciousness and nothing.

Elizabeth called the ambulance. The paramedics used the defibrillator.

I was rushed in for an emergency cesarean.

Twelve hours later, I woke up. Sore. Chest aching. Abdomen burning. Tired. So tired, Lee. But alive.

I think I can tell you now even though you read between the lines before. I didn't know if I would make it. I'm sorry. I won't do that again. I made certain I won't have another pregnancy. This was a one-time thing for me. I suppose it came down to the fact that I don't want to leave the people I love.

And I love you, don't I?

I think I can admit that now. It's not the kind of love you would have for someone you want to marry or that sort of thing. It's not like that.

I don't know exactly what it's like.

Do you have to be able to describe love?

Is it necessary to pin it down and dissect it?

Or can I just say, I care about you, and it feels like—it feels like waking up after passing out on a bed of roses, not knowing if you're going to live or die—you, Lee, feel like waking up. Maybe that's not love, maybe it's something else. But it's how I feel about you.

Maybe that's saying too much.

I'm not asking for anything. God knows you've already done so much. I just want you to know . . . you said that I'm yours. Well, you're mine too.

I named my daughter Louise Gabriel Hobday. Like I said, I received your letter the day she was born. I would have named her Leah, for you, if you hadn't written. But I decided to take your advice and name her Gabriel instead.

I'm out of the hospital. Back home. I've been through this sort of hospital thing before, so I know it might takes months for me to recover.

But in the meantime, I'm going to get to know my daughter. She's two weeks old now. She has soft pink skin, thick black hair like her dad, and muddy eyes that I think will shade to green with time. She's quiet, that's like her dad too, I think. The only time she cries is when she's hungry. Otherwise, she takes in the world with big, wide eyes, searching and curious.

I love her. I told you I would. But Lee, I really love her. When she yawns, my heart cracks open. When she grips my finger with her hand I get tears in my eyes. When she falls asleep, her cheek against my chest, I want to hold her forever. I suppose this feeling is natural, but for some reason, it feels like a miracle.

My mom has forgotten her earlier worries and fears, and she's fallen just as far in love as me. Even my dad, who never really liked babies, holds Louise on his lap and makes funny faces for her.

You'd like her. She's very nonjudgmental. She never discriminates. She lets anyone hold her from the paper boy to those 900 year old grandmas you once met. She'll listen for hours while you talk, and she doesn't mind if your singing voice is off-key. She likes to cuddle. She doesn't complain or whine unless pushed to her limit. She'll hold your hand. She's pure-hearted and I think, she'd remind you of all the good in the world.

So Lee. Thank you. *Thank you.*

In a few months, maybe six, when I'm stronger and everything's in place, Elizabeth and I will start For the Love of Flowers.

I've already found its home. An old brick building downtown next to the chocolate shop. It's been empty since the Holsten's moved their photography studio. But now, it's mine. Ours, if you think of it that way.

Louise and I are going to live upstairs in the two-bedroom apartment. Downstairs we'll have the shop. She'll grow up surrounded by flowers, and my family, and lots of love. It's thanks to you.

So when you're facing darkness, feeling alone, think about us and what you did for us. Think about me, thinking of you.

Do you think, can you call me? If you call my house (not my mobile because I have zero reception in Romeo), someone will pick up and I'll be there, or they'll know where I am. I know it's against the rules we first laid out. But, I very much want to hear your voice. Or email me. Do you want my email? Something that can bridge the silence of the months between letters.

I'm thinking of you.

Merry Christmas.

Happy birthday.

Happy New Year.

Yours,

Cordelia

P.S. I know we said no pictures, but I thought you wouldn't mind a photo of Louise. That's my finger she's holding, and those are my arms cuddling her. I know you didn't ask, but I'll answer. Yes, I'm yours. I'll be yours for as long as you need. Your friend, Cordelia.

four years ago

11

———————

Four years ago

Lee Weston
    c/o I.A.O. West
    514 Hannocks Crossing #2
    Luton, Bedfordshire
    U.K

Dear Lee,

I couldn't wait for your letter. So I'm sending mine. Merry Christmas.

Will you get this in time? I don't know, but I think it will reach you, wherever you are.

I wanted to tell you—we have our tree, an ugly,

scraggly, bent-over Norway spruce. It's probably the ugliest we've ever had. And right on the most bent, most needle-y branch? That's pride of place for the ornament you made.

I let Louise hold your ornament. She showed her appreciation by chewing on the wooden edges of the heart. I laughed because she never gets angry, but when I took away the slobbered-up ornament, she was furious. She balled her hands into fists, arched her back, scrunched up her reddened face and howled. I suppose she likes you as much as I do.

But now it hangs on the tree. Every night, we turn on the colored Christmas lights. It's Louise's favorite thing to do. She watches the lights like they're made of tiny scraps of magic. I'm getting stronger. I'm healing. Even though I haven't slept a full night in months, I'm getting better. Elizabeth and I are opening For the Love of Flowers in the spring.

I wish I could send you a gift. Instead—I made sugar cookies today. Lemon zest, butter, sugar, and glossy royal icing. I made brownies. Double chocolate chip with chopped cherries. A chocolate yule log. And Lee. I made a fruit cake. I made it for you. There isn't anyone else in my life who I would give it to.

Do you hear that? I have made the worst "dessert" known to man just for you. I hope that someday you'll be able to taste it. But in the meantime, know that it's here for you. Just like I am.

Merry Christmas.

Yours,
   Cordelia

~

Dear Lee,

My dad said that a man called the house on Christmas. He said the connection was so poor he could barely make out one word from another. It cut out and dipped between one sentence to the next. But he's certain the man asked for me. And when my dad said I was out ice-skating he said, "Tell Cordelia, Merry Christmas."

Was that you?

I can't stop thinking about it. Was it you? Did you call? Did I miss you by only five minutes? I was already on my way home from the skating pond. Was that you on Christmas? Lee?

I wish . . . well, I wish I'd been there. It hurts to think how close I came to hearing your voice.

I haven't received any letters from you since last summer. Since you wrote me from Bwindi.

I was worried. But then, was that you who called?

I think it was.

I'm waiting on your Christmas card.

Yours,
   Cordelia

~

Dear Lee,

We had our grand opening today. There were more flowers than a garden in full bloom. They spilled from the building onto the sidewalk. I think all of Romeo smelled like a hothouse full of tropical blooms.

We had music, drinks and food, and a great big banner across the front door. Nearly one hundred (a hundred!) people came. My head is spinning, my feet are aching, and I'm absolutely buzzing from it all. I swear I handed out about a thousand business cards.

We had a table where everyone could create their own bouquet and then we wrapped them with twine and glossy brown paper. There were all the spring flowers: colorful gerberas, yellow button poms, white daisies, pink lilies, purple asters, pink and yellow roses, and sprigs of lavender. And for all the tulip lovers, we had more hues of tulips than you could ever imagine. We twined and wrapped more bouquets than I've ever wrapped in my entire life.

It was amazing.

Erma was there, do you remember her? The lady who convinced you to write me? Her best friend Wanda came too. They took fifteen (!) bouquets to share with residents at the retirement home. I think, well, I think Romeo was painted in flowers today. And it's all thanks to you.

Louise and I wore matching pink dresses. They have lace skirts that are frilly and poufy and look like the petals of a rose. Louise had a ribbon in her hair, and my mom spent half the day trying to keep her from putting flower petals in her mouth.

Where are you Lee?

Where in this vast world are you?

I'm still lighting a candle for you. I've created a bouquet for you too. It's full of hibiscus and red roses. I had half a dozen orders for it today. I think it will be a bestseller.

Where are you?

Are you okay?

Yours,

Cordelia

~

Dear Lee,

With summer came a spat of gladiolas and sunflowers. Their stalks long, the flowers nodding in their glass vases. We're busier than I ever imagined. For the Love of Flowers is the only florist in Romeo. Even so, I never could have anticipated how *busy* we would be.

I work with wholesalers to bring in our standing orders once a week. That's the big tubs I told you about— the ones I lug into the cool storage room. We also have a truck that comes twice a week. It's this huge, refrigerated truck that has more flowers to choose from than you could ever imagine. Sometimes I make special orders for weddings, and sometimes I pick out unusual flowers just for fun.

While Elizabeth is still the creative genius of arrangements, I've definitely found my footing. I found it accidentally. We were asked to create a floral arch for a wedding. I stayed up all night sculpting the frame, filling it with greenery and *hundreds* of white roses. My fingers were poked, pinched and a little bloody. But Lee. It was *magical.* I swear. I wrapped the arch in fairy lights and the whole thing looked like something from a fairy tale. After that, everyone wanted a floral arch. I've made tropical arches, pink peony arches, deep red carnation arches. They take so long to make, but they are so beautiful. And I'm proud of them. Really proud.

Maybe that seems funny to you, being proud of flowers. But you should see how happy they make people.

I think you'll be happy to know that we're busy from six in the morning until eight at night. Or maybe you won't be happy and you'll tell me to hurry up and hire more help. To take care of myself. I will. I promise. As soon as I know things really are off the ground.

I'll have a cup of tea. Cuddle on my couch. Read a book I love.

Last week, I did put on a sad movie. One I knew would make me cry. I cried for fifteen minutes and neither Elizabeth or my mom minded because it *was* a sad movie. But Lee. I was crying because . . . I'm scared. It's been a year. Louise's birthday is next week. She's walking. Practically running from room to room. She's saying ma-ma, and mil for milk, and da-da for grandpa, and na-na for grandma, and fi-fi for flower. She loves dogs and birds. She loves flowers. She's still quiet in that way where she takes in everything. She's brave though and her curiosity rules out any caution or fear. She looks more like her dad than me, but I think she has my stubborn streak, it's wide and long. And, it's been a year since your letter. Eight months since your call.

Will I hear from you at Christmas?

Are these letters reaching you?

I can't help thinking that something happened.

Write me.

Yours,

Cordelia

~

Dear Lee,

I finally gave in and called the I.A.O. offices. They wouldn't tell me anything. I'm not family, next of kin, or your emergency contact. But they did tell me that you're still employed there. You're still here, in this world. Would I know it if you were gone? I'd like to believe that I would, but who can really know.

Christmas is almost here. We're selling Christmas bouquets at Romeo's Christmas Market. They're full of crimson amaryllis and pine cones. Poinsettia and holly. Mistletoe and balsam.

I have a fondness for mistletoe. Did I ever tell you that?

This year is our first Christmas in our apartment above the flower shop. I've decorated the entire place with yards of garland, swathes of tinsel, and enough Christmas lights to make night look like day. I play Christmas music nonstop and Louise and I decorated a gingerbread house. Well, I decorated. She ate fistfuls of raisins and smeared frosting on her cheeks. It's cozy and Christmassy, and our tree is ugly with stacks of presents beneath it, and both your ornaments hanging from the boughs. I made you a new fruitcake. I'm not so cruel as to save one over years for you.

Not that I expect you to come. But, it's more . . . I'm thinking of you. Your candle is lit. You're in my heart. Be okay.

Yours,
Cordelia

three years and one month ago

12

THREE YEARS AND ONE MONTH AGO

Cordelia Hobday
 1621 Tenderfoot Lane
 Romeo, NY

Dear Cordelia,

I've wanted to write those two words for so long. Dear Cordelia.

I can't tell you what it means that you're still here, that you're well, that you have a little girl . . . you have no idea how much I held on to that. Or maybe you do, maybe you know exactly what it means. Thank you for staying, for living, for her name. I'm infinitely glad that you're still here.

I'm sitting in the doctor's waiting room, staring at the individual letters of your name. They're different. Can you tell?

You once said you could know someone's character in the way they shaped their words. What does my writing say about me now? It's a messy scrawl. Broken and jagged. The letters fall out of my hand in jagged spurts and interrupted starts.

I think this letter will reach you before Christmas. I could've emailed, called, but I wanted you to see the truth. This letter with its mess of handwriting holds more truth than the neat typing of a keyboard or the muffled lines of a phone could ever convey.

I was always best on the page. It's where you could see me most clearly. But now, the best of me is gone. It was erased, along with everything else.

I wrote you last Christmas, in January, February, March. I think my letters never reached you.

In April, Cruise died. Not telling you about him seems like a betrayal of his life. I don't talk about him though. Not ever. Maybe there is something still there. A line from my heart to my hand. It's my left hand now. Writing with it feels like . . . I'm disconnected. From myself. From you. It doesn't feel like me reaching out anymore.

Almost two years with Cruise. He felt like a brother. He was gruff, quick-tempered. He'd as soon punch you in the face as shake your hand. But those early nights when I was scared, he knew it, and he, well, he never said anything. He'd rip into me about everything else—the flooded roads, the meds, the routes—but he never said anything when I got scared for our lives. We'd hear about aid workers taken, not seen again. He'd just cross himself, then spit in the dirt. He was Catholic like you, he had a tiny rosary in his pocket that he said his kid made for him. I asked him where his family was and he said, "You think I'd be here if I still had one?" He never talked about it again and I never asked.

Then the roads, they flooded. The river swelled. We had this guy from Botswana who taught us how to float our truck across rivers too deep to drive through. We had to get across. You know? We did. We made it. But then, look, it was my choice. I took the wrong route. It was my fault.

When the truck blew, some incendiary in the road, Cruise died right away. Just like that. But me? I hung upside down, wedged in twisted metal, stuck for thirty-six hours while all sorts of creatures came to inspect Cruise and crawl over, never mind, sorry. I'm sorry. I guess the thing is, it took a long time for someone to find us. Then it took eight hours to drive back to a tiny hospital. Then the med evac. Then.

I guess it's not a surprise. You see my writing. My right arm was crushed. I was bleeding out from a gash in my forearm. I took Cruise's belt. I tied my arm off. You know you lose a limb if you don't get the tourniquet off fast enough? Anyway, I spent most of those thirty-six hours unconscious. I only woke up when something big was crawling on us, sniffing the blood.

I'm sorry. I'm sorry I didn't write sooner. I'm sorry. It took a long time to figure myself out. To learn how to write with my left hand. It's a mess, I know.

Please don't worry about me. Please don't. I'm in London for a short break. Before that I was in Malaga. I met someone. Her name is Mara, she was my nurse when I was in intensive care. She's a bit like an angel. I like how calm she is, how nothing seems to bother her. When I was a kid, I used to have this dream that someday someone would take care of me. You know, tuck a blanket up to my chin, brush my forehead when I was tired, bring me a hot bowl of chicken soup when I was sick. I mean, this was a kid's dream. I let go of it a long time ago. But for some reason, I remembered it when she walked into my hospital room. She would change my bandages like none of it bothered her. She would bring meals and be sure to add extra dessert. And when I woke up sweating and my heart pounding, certain I was back, stuck under Cruise, something crawling over us, she'd be there. She'd press her cool fingers to my head and say, *you're alright. It's okay.*

We're getting married next month. Remember I told you I wasn't sure if I knew what love was? I still don't think I do. Mara says she doesn't care, she just wants me. Is that enough? Is that what love is? I think, before, the only person I ever loved was you. But now, it's all jagged and confused. All that light, your candle? It's dark.

Mara asked me not to write you anymore. She saw your letters. She said she doesn't want to compete with you, my "dream girl on a pedestal." That's what she calls you. Is that what you are? Are you just this dream I made up? Are you just like my false brother, my dream family? Someone who isn't real and will just slip away? Lost?

But if you were a dream, I'm glad I had you. So here I am. Trying to let you go. It hurts. I think though, Mara's right. I lost my arm, I lost the route to you, traveling to my heart. You're this phantom, there but not. Neither of us has ever really been there, though, have we?

I'm going to pretend, for just a moment, that I didn't lose my hand and you're still holding it.

Cordelia.

Are you there?

Soon it'll be Christmas. Here's my wish for you. Find someone to love. Find someone who will remember you deserve flowers on Fridays, lemon sugar cookies on Sundays, a stack of books on your nightstand for the weekends. Find someone who cares more about making you smile than anything else. You say that when you find someone to love you won't expect anything in return, you'll just want the gift of loving them. Cordelia, find someone who feels that way about you.

That's my wish for you.

I think . . .

I'll miss you.

When I first wrote, I didn't know who you would be and what you would become. What you would mean to me. We promised to tell the truth. I'm not worthy of you. You see my words. The letters are scarred and ugly. Broken. It's what I've always been. It's just more obvious now.

Cordelia, I want to know that back in Romeo, you're happy. I want to picture you surrounded by flowers. Sunshine. I want to think of you and Louise in your flower dresses. Come Christmas I want to think of you singing your Christmas carols, lighting your candles, untouched by any darkness.

Maybe that's why Mara says you're my dream. You're too beautiful for waking life. You're too beautiful by far.

Don't write, Cordelia. Don't send Christmas cards. Just . . . live. I loved being loved by you, but I can't anymore. You shouldn't either.

I guess, this is the last time I'll say this. Keep it for all the
Christmases.

Merry Christmas, Cordelia.
   Merry Christmas.

—Lee

P.S. I'm returning your lucky penny. It kept me safe, but I
need you to have it now. It was me who called last
Christmas, I'm sorry I didn't get to hear your voice.

~

Lee Weston
   c/o I.A.O. West
   514 Hannocks Crossing #2
   Luton, Bedfordshire
   U.K

Dear Lee,

I wrote a thousand letters. A thousand and one. But I
won't send any of them. You already know what I'm going
to say. The arguments I'd make. The impassioned pleas.
The promises.
   You know me as well as I know myself. Just like I
know you.

You think I don't? You think I can't still see you, even if your letters are broken and jagged? I see you in every crossed t, every circled o, every open u. I'll see you no matter what. Isn't that what we promised?

You know that, though. So I won't tell you the thousand and one things.

Instead, I'll say—

Merry Christmas.

I hope this Christmas and every Christmas from now on is full of joy and love. I hope there are evergreen trees with boughs loaded down with ornaments, the smell of gingerbread and spice, bells ringing and carols sung, the comfort of a home and a love, snow if you have it and sun if you don't, a hand to hold, a gift to give and one to receive, only hellos and never goodbyes, I wish for you, only the happiest of Christmases. Only the happiest, Lee.

Congratulations. You're getting married. Married! For some reason, I never thought about that day. That someday someone would come along and want you all to themselves. I don't blame them. I'd want that too. I understand. I won't stand between you. I want your happiness too.

I want you to know I understand.

But Lee, there's nothing you could do or become that would ever make me stop being your friend. I'm sorry. I'm here. You asked, and I am. I'm here. If you ever need me, write, call, come. Whether it's tomorrow or years away. I'll be here. I'm not a dream. I'm a real person. You know that. I'm as ruined and as broken as the next, but also just as wondrous and unique as everyone else. I'll be here. And if you ever need a place to heal, to just sit quietly and be, then, my flowers are here, and so am I.

Have you noticed that over the years, I added commas

to my life? It's not all short sentences anymore. I take a moment to breathe, and notice, and breathe again, and that's all thanks to you.

I won't write again. At least, I won't put my words to paper. But how can I promise I won't write you when I do that every day? I have been for years.

Thank you for everything you've done for me.

Thank you for being my friend.

Thank you for being by my side for all this time.

Goodbye, Lee, and Merry Christmas.

Merry Christmas, my dearest friend.

Yours,
Cordelia

three years ago

13

———————

THREE YEARS AGO

Dear Lee,

Merry Christmas. I needed to write that down. It felt wrong not to. I'll do better next year.

Yours,
  Cordelia

Unsent

⁓

Dear Cordelia,

~~I miss~~
   ~~I can't~~
   ~~Merry Chr~~

Unsent

two years ago

14

Two years ago

Dear Lee,

Merry Christmas.

Yours,
    Cordelia

Unsent

~

Dear Cordelia,

I won't send this. I only, I want to ask, are you okay? Are you happy? How's Louise? The flowers? Are you laughing? Have you found someone to talk to? Or is it lonely again amid all the people who know you, but don't? Have you found love? I made you an ornament, it's a Christmas rose.

Merry Christmas.

—Lee

Unsent

one year ago

15

———————

One year ago

Cordelia Hobday
   1621 Tenderfoot Lane
   Romeo, NY

Dear Cordelia,

Is it possible to feel like I haven't written those words in a lifetime? Your name? Cordelia.

Can two years without writing you really feel like a hundred?

It's almost Christmas. I think, maybe, this card will surprise you. Then again, maybe it won't. You said you'd always be here and, well, I believed you. And you, maybe you know me better than myself. Maybe you knew what I'd write long before I realized I had to write it.

My stomach is twisting and, I guess, I'm more scared than I've ever been in my entire life. More scared than when I was stuck in that twisted wreck, bleeding out. I'm back in the States, Cordelia. I finally decided it was time for me to come home. Mara left last summer. It turns out, she didn't want me, she wanted, well, the next busted up patient, and after him, she wanted the next. I don't know. I don't blame her. It felt good to be cared for, and I guess it feels good to care for someone else. But it didn't take long for me to realize it wasn't love. Like when I told you that somehow I'd taken a wrong turn and found myself where I wasn't supposed to be? It was like that. I woke up one morning and realized I was living the wrong life.

All those years I was searching for home. I thought I'd find it between here and there. But Cordelia, what if I found it when I was still a kid? What if I left it behind?

It's December. I'm in New York. Last night, the moon was glinting down and these tiny pinpricks of snow started to fall. I didn't know why I booked a ticket to New York. I just felt like I had to come here. I had to see.

When I saw that moon. When I saw the snow. I knew.

All those years, at first I didn't want to care. Then I didn't want to love. Then I did love you, but I thought it wasn't a true kind of love. I didn't think it was the kind of love you have when you want to spend your life with someone.

We've never met.

We've never spoken.

We've never . . .

But after years of losing people I love, after seeing some of the worst of humanity, after having a marriage that was just a photocopy of love, after . . . after missing you for years. I can't miss you anymore.

I'm shaking. I'm scared because what if I'm too late? What if you aren't there anymore? What if you've moved on? What if, like I asked, you found someone to love? What if you don't want to meet me?

But that's why I'm here. I'm in New York City. I guess, I thought, remember when we wrote about spending a day in New York together? Seeing the Christmas decorations, drinking hot cocoa, skating, seeing the Rockefeller tree?

Do you think we could meet for Christmas?

Two years was too long without you. No, it's been nine years without you. I was wrong before, I do know what love is. It's you. It's your words written on my heart. It's me, dragged down by life, but still hoping I make it so someday I can write you again. But now, it's not enough. I want to see you. I want to look into your green eyes and say, "Merry Christmas, Cordelia." Which, if you haven't realized by now, means, I love you.

I love you. It started without me knowing and I've never been able to stop.

Please come to New York. You can meet me in front of the Rockefeller tree. How's 10 a.m. on December 21? You'll recognize me. I'm tall, black haired, brown eyed. Just like I always said, I look both older and meaner than I am. I'll be the one holding a bunch of red roses and hibiscus in my left hand. Like you said, I should only give hibiscus to someone I love. Passionately.

Well, that's you. I love you passionately. I'd like . . . do you think I could see your shop? Sit and take in the flowers? Meet your daughter? See your Hobday Christmas?

I'm done running. I'm done searching. The only place I want to run is to you.

You can send your reply to this address. It's the hotel where I'm staying. After that . . . we'll see. I guess it depends on you.

I've realized that I'll do whatever you want or need. Anything. So if you don't want to meet, that's okay. If you don't want to write, okay. If you come to New York, see me from afar, and then realize I'm not . . . just not who you want. Then that's okay. If that's the case, I won't write again.

But I'm here, and I can't go another day without knowing. Write me. Tell me if I should wait under the Christmas tree with a handful of hibiscus and roses.

Merry Christmas, Cordelia.

—Lee

~

Lee Weston
    Two East 55th Street
    New York, NY
    10022

Dear Lee,

Yes. I'm coming. You're not too late. I'm coming.
Merry Christmas. Merry Christmas, Lee.

Yours,
    Cordelia

16

New York, NY
December 21

Cordelia

Corey left Romeo when the sky was still veiled in black and lit with the iridescent tinsel of glittering stars. The moon was full and cast a silver light over the town's frost-coated evergreens, the sleepy houses, and the quietly blinking stoplight on Main Street. The air was so cold her breath puffed out in front of her and the frosted puddles on the ground cracked under her feet.

It was the time of morning when the night owls had finally gone to sleep, and the morning birds hadn't yet awakened. It was so quiet the rumble of her engine echoing across the brick buildings of downtown Romeo sounded like they would echo all the way to New York

City. It was so cold she rubbed her hands together and blew on them because her heater hadn't warmed up yet. It was so dark she'd have to drive at least three hours until she saw a hint of the sun.

All the same, she would've left earlier. She'd *wanted* to.

In fact, she didn't sleep at all. She spent the entire night tossing and turning, then pacing, then baking a tray of brownies, a fruit cake, and finally lemon zest sugar cookies. Then, when it was still only three in the morning she went downstairs and put together a Christmas basket full of every flower that meant friendship and love.

At four, she took a shower then dried and curled her hair and put on makeup. Then she put on a black sheath dress, took it off, put on a red skirt with a green cardigan, took it off, put on jeans with a blue wool sweater, took it off, then put the black sheath back on with black wool tights and black boots.

At four thirty, her mom pulled into the parking spot in front of the shop. She let herself in and when she saw Corey, she shook her head.

"Are sure about this?"

"Yes," Corey answered before her mom even stopped speaking.

"You've never met him. You're running to the city, your heart in your hands. You don't know him—"

"I know him better than I've known anyone in my life."

"And you don't know if he's who he says he is." They'd already had this conversation the night before. Although then the whole family had been there for it. Lee's letter had come to her parents' house, and her mom had given it to her before the family dinner. "Corey. He could be anyone. He could be a sixty-year-old woman with a pruning shear fetish. Or a fifty-year-old man with a criminal record. Or—"

"Or he could be Lee. My best friend. Who I've loved for nine years."

Corey looked down at the basket of flowers in one hand, and the box with the fruit cake, cookies, and brownies in the other. Her hand trembled, so she curled it more tightly around the wicker handle. Her heart fluttered, only a little, like a bird's wing tapping against a windowpane. It had been flying like that since she'd received his letter.

He loved her. He wanted to meet her.

"Just be careful. For me."

Corey nodded. She couldn't stop her mom from worrying. There wasn't anything that could stop that.

"I will." She looked out the window at the streetlights shining over the sleeping town. Her breath was tight, her muscles tense. She felt like someone at the starting block, just waiting for the gunshot. She wanted to go. Run. "I put out cereal for Louise. She only gets one cup of juice, no matter what she says. She'll want to stay at the playground for hours, but if it gets too cold—"

"I know. I've watched her about . . . hmm . . . fifty thousand times. We'll be fine, Corey. You on the other hand? Don't feel like you have to say hello if he doesn't look like someone you'd like."

"You know I don't care what he looks like."

"Or if he has a bad, mean-eyed kind of look. Or if he's just . . . odd. Just leave. You can—"

"Mom." Corey leaned forward and pressed a kiss to her mom's cheek. Her mom's skin was still cold from the early December morning wind, and she smelled like snow and hand-knitted wool. Corey smiled as she rested her cheek against her mom's. "I'm going now."

"You're sure?"

Corey nodded. She'd been sure for so long.

"I'm sure. I'm really, really sure."

Her mom gave her a tight squeeze. "Then I can't wait to meet him."

After that, Corey tiptoed into Louise's bedroom, kissed her goodbye—careful not to wake her—and began the long drive south to the city.

She sped down the black ribbon of road that twisted through pine forests, evergreen-topped mountains, and deep lakes that reflected the stars. The night gave way to a pink-kissed dawn. The sun reflected off the gold-tinged, frost-coated glass buildings of Albany. But almost before she noticed them, she was past the capital and speeding south. She followed the Hudson, the mountains had smoothed out into hills, and the hills had smoothed out into boulder-strewn forests.

All the while, Corey gripped the wheel tightly. Her skin was flushed, buzzing, her heart had moved from flutters to a tumbling hummingbird whir that pulsed in her ears.

She didn't listen to music, the only sound was her tires on the road, the wind whistling over her car's hood, and the whoosh of passing cars and semis. She kept the temperature cold so that she'd stay awake. She leaned forward, like her body was trying to pull ahead of her car.

Lee.

In a few hours she'd see Lee.

His name was a pulse in her blood. The sound of her beating heart. She didn't know what today would bring. But she did know one thing. She would hug him. She would hold him in her arms. She would run across Rockefeller Plaza, right under that Christmas tree, and she would wrap her arms around him. And just . . . just hold him. For minutes. For hours. She didn't know. She only knew that she'd hold him. And then she'd take his hand. Maybe they'd walk the city. Maybe they'd talk. Maybe he'd eat the fruit cake she'd made him. Or maybe . . . maybe they'd do more.

Would he kiss her?

Would he still love her when he saw her?

Would the connection they felt on paper be there in life?

She knew his heart. Would she still recognize it in person?

She would. She knew she would.

At nine the traffic thickened. Stop and go. A slow crawl. The George Washington Bridge was ahead, towering over the Hudson. It spanned the river, connecting New Jersey to New York. Thousands of cars merged and jockeyed and honked. Corey stared at the wide, ice-blue river, and across it, the city and the silver skyscrapers glinting into the rising sun and the pale morning sky.

Lee was somewhere in that city. He was there right now. Maybe he was already at Rockefeller. Maybe, like her, he hadn't been able to sleep. Or maybe he was buying the roses and hibiscus, so she'd recognize him right away.

It was nine thirty, after she'd crossed the bridge and moved into New York traffic, when her phone rang. It was her brother, John.

"Corey. You have to come back—"

Her breath was a quick, indrawn knife.

"What? Louise?"

"No. It's Mom."

After living a life of hospitals and emergencies and lowered voices, Corey knew that something was wrong. Terribly wrong.

Her family had spoken about her in that tone of voice enough times that she *knew*.

Her hands shook as she swerved to the right, took the exit, and pulled to the side of the road, double parking. She put on her emergency flashers and ignored the cars honking behind her.

"You have to come. The doctor doesn't know—"

The pounding of her pulse rushed in her ears. John's voice faded in and out. Elizabeth had found her mom when she came into work at nine. Louise had stumbled down to the shop crying. Her mom had a stroke while making Louise breakfast. She hit her head on the counter when she fell. She hadn't regained consciousness. It was doubtful that she would.

Corey couldn't understand. The words were there. John was speaking in clear, slow sentences, but she couldn't seem to piece together what he was saying.

Her mom . . .

Her mom?

He was saying her mom . . . their mom . . . who had always been there and who was supposed to be there for decades more was . . . not?

Suddenly. Unexpectedly. Not?

Corey's hands were tight on the wheel, and her breath came in short, tight gasps. The sky was a bright, winter blue, even while it seemed like it should be cracking and breaking apart, falling into gray.

"They don't think she'll make it. Corey, the doctor said if you want to say goodbye, you—"

A small strangled sound escaped her. How could there be a day where in the morning her mom was there and then by night, she wasn't? How could her mom move from always there by her side to used to be, once was, gone?

To someone only spoken of in the past tense.

She'd never realized before how the past tense could break someone's heart.

Love to loved.

Know to knew.

Have to had.

Corey stared at the crowded road, the honking cars swerving around her, the line of vehicles moving south toward the city, toward Rockefeller.

For a split second, she thought about the Christmas tree there. Her best friend waiting to meet her. If she didn't come, would he write her? Would he come to Romeo and find her? She needed him. Right now, she needed him desperately. She needed him to hold her hand.

But maybe, when she didn't come, he'd think that she didn't want him after all. Was this where it ended?

"How long?" Corey's voice came out overloud, and she flinched.

A truck honked behind her, and she gripped the steering wheel more tightly, her hands shaking. She tasted the salty copper of blood and realized she was biting her lip so hard she'd broken skin.

"Hours. Less. I don't know. I have to go. The doctor's back. Hurry, Mom would want . . . hurry, Corey."

John was gone. She was left in the tomb of her car, the traffic impatient behind her, swerving around her.

There was something wrong with her. Something very wrong. There were black wings at the edge of her vision, and she couldn't get a breath. Her heart pounded, a silent drum, aching and undone.

A sharp line of sweat formed on her upper lip, and her mouth went numb.

Her mom . . . her mom who always worried that she would lose her daughter. Corey couldn't move. She couldn't think. The pain and fear of it was clawing at her and scratching her insides. She couldn't do this.

Right now, she didn't even know if she could breathe.

Then suddenly, she remembered what she'd once written Lee. *If you're afraid, then let the fear in. Let it devour you. Let it do its worst. And once it's had all of you, it will leave. Then you can make room for other emotions.*

So Corey let the fear consume her. That today, she was saying goodbye to her mom. But she was also saying goodbye to Lee. Because there was no telling what he'd do or where he'd go. He'd said if she wasn't there, he'd understand that she didn't want him. He wouldn't write again.

But she couldn't think about that. Right now, she had to reach her mom. She couldn't let her go without saying goodbye. It all hinged on that. A goodbye. Her mom had loved her too much, had given her too much love. Corey had always felt that way. She had to go to her. Either to be there to help her live or to be there to help her die. Corey knew a lot about both, and her mom needed her now.

It didn't matter that this was unexpected. That hours ago, her mom was fine and now . . . she'd think about that later. All that mattered was reaching her.

With that decided, the fear peeled back. The wings at the edge of her vision flew away. The city reformed, the brown brick buildings, the stone bridges over the street, the cars honking as they flew past. The fire hydrants, the metal gates over the closed shops, and the bare December trees.

Corey pulled in a jagged breath, broke her lip free of her teeth, loosened her hands on the wheel, turned off her flashers, and put the car back into drive.

She gave one final look toward the city, where she knew Rockefeller was. He was there. She knew.

He was there with roses and hibiscus in his hand.

Corey's hands trembled on the wheel.

"Please," she whispered, her throat tight and aching, "please."

She didn't know whether she was saying please for her mom, to make it to Romeo in time, or for Lee to write her again, to find her and hold her. Maybe it was for all three.

"I love you." Her voice broke on the words.

Then she pulled back into traffic, turned her car around, and drove away from the city.

This was goodbye.

Her heart wasn't fluttering, pounding, or galloping. It couldn't. It was broken.

17

———

New York, NY
December 21

Lee

She'd said yes. Lee had never been so happy in his life as the moment he received Cordelia's letter at the hotel's front desk and read the word—*yes*.

There were other happy moments, sure. Learning to carve his first wooden ornament, finding out that he was smart enough to read and write, cold winter mornings with Saul and Jackson, chocolate yule log cake with a funny, beautiful girl and then years later meeting her again and making love, jokes with Cruise, that first dance with Mara.

But most of his happy moments were twined with Cordelia's letters. Her words weaving through his years. It was like her letters were all lined up, stringing together the days of his life, and things only made sense through the flow of her words.

She made him laugh, made him smile, made him love.

At first he hadn't recognized the feeling he got when he held her letters. His skin buzzed, his insides vibrated, his heart pulse with incandescence. Whenever he held her letters the weight of his past fell away and he flew. He was light. It took him years to figure it out, but now he knew that feeling was love.

So when he read her words—*yes. I'm coming. You're not too late. I'm coming.*

Merry Christmas. Merry Christmas, Lee—he felt it again. That lightness of being.

So on December 21 at six in the morning, Lee walked with a springing, happy, light stride toward Rockefeller Plaza. He couldn't help the smile that clung to his lips. He'd been awake all night. There was no way that he would sleep. He was finally going to meet her. Cordelia. She said he wasn't too late. She'd said—*Merry Christmas.*

He wasn't tired. His blood pumped with enough adrenalin to keep him awake for days. He'd been dreaming about this moment for, to be honest, years.

Some nights, years past, he'd lain awake, staring at the ceiling or the open sky, and imagine her there with him. She'd tell him about her family, her flowers, her daughter. Sometimes if it had been a hard day, she wouldn't say anything. She'd just lie next to him and hold his hand.

But that was his dream of her. This? Today? This was real. He'd take a real Cordelia over his dreams any day.

He had a bouquet of a dozen red roses and bloom

after bloom of red hibiscus. It was so she'd recognize him in the crowd of people pushing together to see the giant Christmas tree.

For a minute, he worried that when she saw him she'd be disappointed. He was worse for wear. A lot worse. But then he shook it off because worrying about something like that wasn't facing facts. The facts were he was who he was. Cordelia was who she was. Looks, bodies, appearances—when had any of that mattered to them? Not once.

So he shrugged off the worry and kept on to Rockefeller. On the way, he found a bakery and bought a half-dozen muffins. He bought chocolate chip, lemon blueberry, cherry with cinnamon crumble, pumpkin spice, apple, and banana because he didn't know what she'd like best, but he figured she might be hungry when she arrived.

He made it to Rockefeller Plaza by seven fifteen, just in time to watch the sun rise. The golden strands of light peeked over the eastern horizon and combed the sky with feathery pink and orange clouds.

The sky went from the soft muted indigo of night in the city to the cornflower blue of winter dawn. The plaza was quiet, the silver metal and glass reflected the sunrise, and the only noise was the distant rumble of the subway, far off, the sound of early traffic, and the quiet cooing of pigeons collecting around the remains of a bagel.

Lee tilted his head back and followed the boughs of the Christmas tree skyward. The white gold lights were always shining, all 50,000 of them, and in the dawn light, they were glowing like stars in the sky. He smiled and he felt the smile from the tips of his fingers all the way to his toes.

She'd said yes.

It was seven thirty, but maybe she'd be early. Maybe she hadn't been able to sleep, just like him. Besides, he didn't mind waiting.

Years ago, he'd always thought the Rockefeller tree was where he'd lost his family. Now, he didn't know if that was true. Maybe he did let go of his brother's hand here. Or maybe that memory wasn't real. Maybe he'd never know. This place had always represented the loss of family to him. But now it represented something else. This was where he would meet Cordelia.

At eight, he bought a coffee from a food truck.

At eight thirty, he gave a homeless man with a shivering chihuahua twenty dollars.

At nine, he read Cordelia's letter again. Just to make sure that he'd read it right. That she had said yes.

At nine fifteen, the plaza was full of people, hurrying to work, dropping kids at daycare, shopping at the plaza stores, taking pictures of the tree, touring the city.

At nine forty-five, he studied every person who walked toward the tree. He was looking for a woman who was shorter than average, with green eyes the color of a balsam forest, and a love of flowers.

At ten, he stood beneath the Christmas tree, the shadow of the boughs over him. The winter breeze tugged at his hair, and he thought maybe he should've worn a coat. He'd never needed anything but a flannel before, but years in tropical and desert climates may have changed his internal temperature.

Still, he waited, the flowers held tight in his hand, a hopeful smile on his face, his gaze searching the people zigzagging through the plaza. He'd see her any minute.

Any second she'd be here. His breath came out in short puffs in front of him and his heart pounded in his ears.

He couldn't wait. How had he waited this long? Years. He'd waited *years*.

At ten fifteen he asked a man passing by for the time. Maybe because he'd been abroad, he hadn't updated his phone and watch properly, and he had the hour wrong.

"Ten fifteen."

At ten thirty, he asked a woman in a puffy black coat what the date was. Maybe he was a day early.

"The twenty-first."

At eleven, his hand was cramped from holding the roses so tightly. Their sweet fragrance filled the air, mixing with the scent of frost-coated concrete, subway steam, and car exhaust. There had been a steady stream of people coming and going. Some paused to look up at the tree, others ignored it completely. No one looked at him.

At noon, the sun was high overhead. The sky was a washed-out blue with no clouds and no snow. The wind whistled around the buildings and shook the branches of the Christmas tree. The lights tinkled together with every shivery breeze and let out a sort of dull thudding music.

"You got another dollar?" This was at twelve thirty.

Lee gave the homeless man with the chihuahua all the cash in his wallet.

At one, he took three minutes and thirty seconds to buy another coffee. He held the flowers under his arm, put the box of muffins on a ledge of concrete, and sipped the hot, bitter drink.

There was plenty to see. Awestruck, slack-jawed tourists. Hurrying, hard-jawed New Yorkers. Shops with spectacular Christmas window displays. Ice-skating.

Christmas trees. Art Deco architecture. There was so much bustle around him. Lee blocked it all out. He didn't want to be distracted. He didn't want to miss her.

At four, the sun had started its downward slant, and the afternoon traffic picked up, preparing for rush hour as people pushed past. He was tired. His eyes were gritty. Not sleeping and not eating had finally caught up with him. The flowers were starting to wilt. The hibiscus especially. The tropical flower wasn't meant to stay out so long in the bitter cold.

Lee lifted the lid of the bakery box. He stared down at the muffins. Which one would be Cordelia's least favorite? She'd love the chocolate. He thought she'd probably like the lemon blueberry. Maybe . . . maybe she didn't like banana. He ate the banana muffin then closed the lid.

At four thirty, the sun set. It was a quick, dying gasp. For a moment, the sky was lit and then it wasn't anymore. After that, it was a sort of half light. Lee kept under the Christmas tree, standing under the 50,000 lights. He wondered how long it would take to count them.

At six fifteen, he went into a diner, bought a soup to go, and was back outside by six twenty. He'd decided that Cordelia probably thought that he'd written ten p.m.

New York was beautiful at night. The tree lights would shine so bright. She'd come. He was sure of it.

At eight, he rested against the cold, flat gray stone of the building overlooking the tree, the sculpture above staring at the tree with him. There was laughter from the nearby ice-skating rink, the sharp shout of a taxi horn, and the excited burr of tourists admiring the tree. He closed his eyes, but only for a moment.

At ten, the plaza was quiet again. Only a few people walked through, and none of them were looking for him.

Over the day the people had become faceless again. He was on his own. Once again his hand was empty and he'd let go. Well, was it him that had let go? Was it ever him?

She wasn't coming.

Or maybe she had come and she'd seen him and she'd decided . . . he wasn't what she'd imagined. Or who she'd imagined.

Or . . .

At midnight, he set the bouquet of roses and hibiscus at the base of the Christmas tree.

He dropped the muffins next to the homeless man with the chihuahua.

At his hotel, he asked if there were any letters for him. There weren't. Any phone calls? No. Did anyone stop by and ask for him? Not that either.

In the morning, after a half-sleepless night, Lee decided that Cordelia wouldn't have said she'd come and then . . . not. And if she had seen him and decided she didn't want to know him, she would've let him know. Somehow.

He called the Hobday phone number, the one for her family home that he'd called years ago.

He just . . . wanted to make sure.

"'Lo?" It was a young girl, maybe a teen, maybe younger.

"Hi. This is Lee Weston. I'm calling for Cordelia Hobday."

"Ummm. You mean . . ."

Lee gripped the phone. The last time he'd called Cordelia, her dad had answered, but now it was

December 22 and maybe all her relatives had started to pile into the old house. If this girl was a young cousin, he might have to be more specific.

"Louise's mom. David's daughter. Cordelia Hobday?"

"Oh. Ohhhh. No, she's not here." The little girl was barely speaking above a whisper. Lee had to strain to hear her.

"Is she at her flower shop?"

"I don't know."

Lee realized, quite suddenly, that his stomach had fallen to the floor. His breath came out in a rush. He hadn't quite acknowledged that he'd been afraid something had happened to her. But if something had, then this girl would've said so.

"Do you know," he asked carefully, his grip tight on the room phone, "if she went to New York City yesterday?"

"Uh-huh. But she came back right away."

Lee stared at the far wall of his hotel room. The lines of the wallpaper blurred into a single gray mass. The lamp light faded in and out. He struggled for a second to realize what exactly she was saying.

But if he hadn't believed her words, he could believe the feeling overcoming his body. It was a tight, pained lurching in his chest. An ache that traveled from the place where his hand used to be, up his arm, into his chest. It spiked him there, a sharp burst of pain in his heart.

So she'd come. She'd said she would. She came to New York. And then she left.

While he stood under the tree, his heart in his hand, she turned around and left.

"Tell her . . ." Lee cleared his throat. There was a

burning at the back of his eyes and a clawing in his throat. He spoke through it. "Please tell her . . . I'm sorry. It's okay. I won't write again. No, just tell her—"

"I don't know, mister. I probably can't remember all that."

Lee pushed back a raw laugh. He could picture it. The house full of people, everyone crowded together, the sugar cookies and hot cocoa at the front door, the tilting tree, and the carols plunked out on the piano. This kid was one of Cordelia's multitude of Hobdays.

"That's alright. Just tell her Lee said . . . Merry Christmas."

After Lee hung up, he sat in the quiet of his hotel room. It was silent like the deep winter woods, quiet like a forest cabin in the night, still like the stars as you waited for someone to find you bleeding out in a truck, and well, it was lonely.

Lee hadn't been lonely like this in nine years. Since that time before when he hadn't had anyone. Since before Cordelia. He'd forgotten what it felt like to be completely without her.

What would he do now?

What did a man do when everything he put his hope into died? What did he do when he was alone and his dreams were long gone?

What did he do, and where did he go?

He turned from the blank shadowed wall and looked out the window toward the Christmas lights strung on the building across the street.

He stared at the lights until they blurred and bobbed in front of him. Finally, the heater clicked on and a rustle of air brought him back to the small room. The crumpled sheets, the scent of roses still lingering, the coffee maker full of used grounds. His suitcase with all his worldly possessions propped on the floor.

It was almost Christmas.

What was it that Christmas meant to him?

Lee packed his bag, zipped it closed. Turned off the lights of his hotel room. Checked out and left New York City. This time, he knew, there wasn't anything for him there. There wasn't any reason for him to ever come back.

Cordelia
Romeo, NY

When Corey's ten-year-old second-cousin Janna told her Lee had called, Corey almost collapsed with relief. She hadn't slept in two days. Her mom was gone. Louise was a wreck. She was a wreck but she was trying to tie it up tight, box it all inside, and hold it together for her daughter and her family.

But Lee.

He'd called. He hadn't left or given up on her or anything like that. He'd . . . called.

But then Janna couldn't remember what he'd said, except Merry Christmas. That's all. Merry Christmas.

Still. He'd called, and that meant he'd call again. Or he'd write. Or . . . he'd come.

But he didn't.

Corey, her dad, and her siblings had a funeral to plan for her mom. She stayed up for hours making the floral arrangements for the casket and the church. Not because anyone had asked but because she had to. She wanted to do one last thing for her mom.

Everyone was there. All the Hobdays came for Christmas and they all would stay for the funeral. Just like she'd told Lee. She was surrounded by a hundred people and she couldn't talk to any of them. She needed to help her dad, comfort her daughter, hold her at night when she woke up crying for her nana. She had to help with the funeral arrangements and make sure that Christmas was still happy for her younger cousins.

On Christmas Eve, when Louise was finally asleep, Corey held a pen tightly in her grip and wrote a letter she desperately prayed would somehow reach Lee. She didn't know where to send it, so she'd mail it to London and hope they forwarded it on. She knew it wouldn't happen, but still, she prayed.

She furiously brushed the tears from her cheeks and wrote—

Dear Lee,

I know this Christmas card will never reach you.

I know these words will never find you.

I know each word I write pulls me further away from you. As if each letter is another beat in time, pushing us apart.

But if I could have one Christmas wish come true, it would be you.

Somehow, the Christmas cards I wrote became pieces of my soul addressed to you. I didn't mean to love you, but that's what happened.

I love you.

I need you.

Please.

I need you.

If somehow this letter can fly off the page and find its way to your heart—

I need you.

Find me in Romeo. Find me at Christmas.

Yours,
　　Cordelia

If there was any Christmas magic left, then he'd come.

On January 12th, she found her letter in the mailbox. Stamped on the envelope were the words *Return to Sender, Postage Due.*

He wasn't coming.

That night, Corey put on a sad movie and no one questioned why she cried.

this Christmas

18

This Christmas . . .

Romeo, NY
    December 22

Lee

The cold air curled around Lee as he stared out over downtown Romeo. It was exactly as he remembered it, even though he'd only been once, ten years ago this Christmas. Snow piled around him, mounded at the edge of the street and scraped from the sidewalk into little sledding hills at the edge of yards. There was a snowman with a lopsided carrot for a nose at the end of the block, and a yard full of grown-up snow angels with kid-size snow angels next to them.

The air was full of Christmas, that fir and evergreen scent that always pulled at something in his chest. The wind bit at his cheeks and stirred the snow in little swirling eddies so that tiny flakes slipped down his boots and past his pulled-up collar. They melted against his skin in bursts of icy cold.

Romeo was quaint. Quintessentially Christmas. Down the street, he could hear the Christmas Market. There was the hum of the classic Christmas songs and the noise of people laughing, all of it muffled by the blanket of snow.

He knew there'd be Christmas trees for sale along the sidewalk, real reindeer to pet, and booths full of wreaths, gifts, and peppermint hot cocoa.

Everywhere he looked there were Christmas lights, sparking and shining off the layer of fresh snow. He was a few blocks east of downtown and the Christmas Market. The music and the sight of the decorated wooden booths called him forward, but he stayed where he was.

1621 Tenderfoot Lane.

The house was exactly like Cordelia described. It looked just like the photo she'd sent. It was an old Victorian elegantly sliding tipsily to the side, a little wobbly and knee-bent but full of charm. It was painted cloud pink, baby blue, lilac, and sage green, with butter yellow trim and bright-pink shutters. Maybe all the Hobdays had chosen their favorite color, and this was the result.

There was a white picket fence covered with puffs of snow. A bird feeder hung next to the fence where a bright red cardinal perched on the loft, piping a quick song.

There was the giant rose bush with tightly closed rose hips coated in frost. Snow mounded over the bush, and icicles dangled from the branches. There was a wraparound porch for sitting on in the summers. There was a tall chimney for fires in the winter. There was an old oak tree for jumping in leaves in the fall. He knew, automatically, that under the snow were flower bulbs waiting to bloom in the spring.

This was where Cordelia grew up, and this was where all the Hobdays congregated for Christmas.

Lee looked up at the candles glowing in the windows and felt the reflection of a warm hope spreading through him. There was something about the single lights set in each window that felt like he was being called home.

It was true. He felt suddenly as if he'd come home.

He'd stayed away for a year. He hadn't written. He hadn't called. Instead, he'd thought about where he wanted to go, what he wanted to do, and who he wanted to become.

He'd wondered for a time, about Christmas. Why it meant so much to Cordelia and why it meant so much to him. Then, on a dark, cold night, sitting out watching the first star blink to life, he realized what it was. Christmas came at the darkest, coldest time of year. The shortest, darkest days. Wasn't Christmas the reminder that even in the dark and the cold, there was still hope?

He thought about that for a long time. He'd never admitted this, but when he was fourteen, and he'd first written Cordelia, he was losing faith in himself and in the world. He was, for lack of a better word, in the dark. Then there she was. She was love, and even if he didn't know it right away, that's what she'd always been. So every Christmas, no matter how hard or how dark the world was, he reminded himself of the light.

Merry Christmas.

Merry Christmas, he'd said.

But Merry Christmas had always been a simpler way of saying I love you.

So each year, on his own, or struggling to survive, he'd reach out for Cordelia and Christmas. Once he realized that, he knew what he wanted to do. For the next year, he drew up plans, found contractors and suppliers, and then began production on hand-carved, one-of-a-kind, keepsake Christmas ornaments.

The ornaments were beautiful works of art. He knew each one would bring happiness and wonder to anyone who held it. Each of them had a little bit of Christmas magic in them. He decided early on that the proceeds would go to IAO and the people still working to spread aid around the world.

So here he was, knowing exactly where he was and what he was doing.

Except, for the past year, while he was pulling himself together, he'd missed Cordelia. She was a part of him, and it's never easy to let go of a part of yourself.

In fact, he hadn't let go. It wasn't something he'd been capable of. So he decided that for one more Christmas, he'd hold a candle in his heart and reach out his hand.

Christmas had always been their time. So for one last Christmas, he'd written a letter. Except this time, he'd come to Romeo with it.

Lee walked through the gate, a puff of snow blowing out before him. His cheeks were cold and probably red, his dark hair windblown. His gaze flickered to the candle in the window by the front door. It was a steady luminescence.

Cordelia's front porch smelled like cinnamon spice and evergreens with just a touch of lemon. There was a large wreath on the front door full of golden ribbons and poinsettias. Two urns full of red, white, and green Christmas flowers stood next to the front door.

Would there be Hobdays inside? A cavalcade of them racing up and down the stairs, banging on the piano, cooking burnt Christmas dinners? Or would they all be at the Christmas Market or skating at the pond?

He restrained a smile and knocked on the door.

He waited, resisting the urge to fidget and fighting the nerves jumping over him and rolling around in his chest. Would she be happy to meet him? Would she be upset? Would she . . .

"They aren't home."

It was a high, creaky voice shouted from the sidewalk over the picket fence.

Lee turned around and took in a small, white-haired woman, huddled in a green parka, with a holly berry hat and a yellow lab in a Christmas scarf. The dog was sniffing the snowbank, ignoring him, but the woman waved him away from the house.

"None of them are home. What do you have? Christmas cookies?"

She looked hopefully at the white box with the red ribbon in his hand. It had his letter tucked under the ribbon and the ornament he first carved after leaving New York.

Lee stepped down from the porch, careful of the thin sheet of ice coating the sidewalk. He smiled at the reminder of Cordelia slipping and falling years ago on the ice coating the mud.

He smiled at the woman. The yellow lab finally noticed him. The dog wagged his entire body as he sniffed Lee's boots.

She hmphed, then said, "You can probably leave those on the porch. The cold'll keep them fresh. Or . . . I could take them. I'd only eat a few."

She gave him a dimpled smile.

Lee laughed, forgetting how tight his chest was and how his stomach had twisted with nervousness only seconds before.

"I actually . . . I'm looking for Cordelia Hobday." He took a breath. Smiled. "Do you know where I could find her? Is she—"

Lee cut off at the look on the woman's face. She'd taken a sharp, quick breath. All the pink went out of her cheeks and her wrinkles which he hadn't really noticed before, became heavy and weighted down until she looked even older than she could possibly be. It was as if the laughter had been blown out by a sharp, cold gust of wind.

"Cordelia?" Her voice was soft, not a creaky hinge anymore, but a weighted bough sighing in the wind.

For some reason Lee didn't want to answer her. He wanted to take a step back, and another, and then another until he was away from this woman with her pitying expression. She laid her hand on the sleeve of his flannel and shook her head.

"Yes. Cordelia Hobday." His throat was closing. She kept patting his arm as if she had something she didn't want to say.

"I'm sorry. Cordelia's gone. You didn't know?"

There was a rushing in Lee's ears. A howling he didn't know how to stop. It was a sound that came from outside of him but inside as well.

"She's not in Romeo?" His voice was hollow and far off.

The yellow lab sniffed at him, nudged his thigh and whined. The woman squeezed his arm.

"No dear, Cordelia died. We were all so shocked. It was sudden and her poor family, for it to happen at Christmas, well, it isn't the sort of thing—"

"What did you say?" He couldn't quite understand. She was speaking. Her mouth was moving. There were words coming out, but he couldn't understand them.

He thought she'd said that Cordelia was dead. But Cordelia couldn't be dead. She was his. She'd always been his. He loved her and . . .

She'd loved him, hadn't she?

She was here in Romeo. For Christmas. For always. She was his light home.

It didn't matter what happened last year. It didn't matter what they'd done or not done. It didn't matter that time and space had separated them. They'd been each other's from the start.

It wasn't possible that she'd left and he didn't know it. He would've felt the flame of her candle go out. Wouldn't he?

She'd promised, hadn't she? She'd promised to be his friend for as long as she lived.

And he'd promised her.

He stared at the empty house and the candles shining in the windows. The cold cut him and sank into him. He was certain the woman was still talking, but all he could hear was the howling of the wind.

There was a cracking, a great wrenching inside him, and it felt as if he was splitting apart.

"When?" he turned to the woman, his voice harsh.

"Sorry?"

"When did it happen?"

"Oh . . ." The woman set her hand on her dog's head and looked up at the pearly blue sky, counting back. "It was before Christmas. The twenty-first? The twenty-second? I'm sorry, I can't remember. You knew her?"

Lee stared at the woman, the date ringing around in his head. He'd been waiting for her under the Rockefeller Christmas tree, and she'd . . .

Been hurt?

Known she was sick?

Rushed home?

Because she'd come. The girl on the phone had told him that she'd come to New York, and then . . . she died?

The woman shifted under Lee's stare and then tugged at her dog's collar, urging him along. "I'm sorry I had to be the one to tell you."

Lee could only feel a numbness spreading out from his chest and reaching down his arm, down his legs. It was the numbness you get when you've been out in the cold, and your body has given up the fight for feeling.

"It's okay." Even though it wasn't, it wouldn't ever be okay. "It's fine."

She patted his arm one more time and sent him a sympathetic smile.

As she turned to go, Lee asked, "How did she die?"

"A stroke. Did you know her very well?"

Lee felt the numbness reach every part of him, even the fingers on his left hand. The letter under his fingers was cold, the words empty now.

"I was her friend."

"Ah. Well. I hope you can still have a Merry Christmas."

Lee stared after the woman as she walked her dog

down the sidewalk, letting him sniff every mailbox and fencepost buried by the snow.

He couldn't feel his body. He was floating outside of himself in a rushing wind. It was howling and frigid cold.

Cordelia was gone. She'd gone and left him.

She'd left him, and he hadn't known. He knew with a deep certainty that Cordelia was it for him. There wouldn't be any other love. There wouldn't be any other flame or candle burning across the world, hoping to guide him home. She was the one who fit the jagged edges of his soul, and with her gone, he'd spend the rest of his life with a piece of himself missing.

He came here today to see if she could want him. He'd been praying for a bit of Christmas magic. He'd wondered if maybe last year at Rockefeller was a mistake, and he could convince her that she'd like him in person if only she gave him a chance.

He had a letter.

He had himself.

He'd come prepared for her to say goodbye. But he hadn't prepared for her to be gone already with no chance of ever saying goodbye.

Lee sank to the icy sidewalk, dropped his head to his knees, and wept.

19

Cordelia

It was Christmas in Romeo, and Corey was the bloom in the center of all the Christmas cheer. There wasn't any place like a small town at Christmas, and there especially wasn't any place like Romeo at Christmas. She knew this. She was a Hobday after all. So even if she'd wanted to escape the cheer, which she *didn't*, she wouldn't have been able to anyway.

For weeks, she'd lived and breathed a flower shop stuffed to the brim with the heady scent of fir and cedar garlands, the bright red and white of blooming poinsettias, the cinnamon stick and star anise spice of homemade wreaths.

For the Love of Flowers was small, a square little front room with a checkerboard floor, old cherry wood built-in shelves, a tin ceiling, and wrought-iron café tables stuffed with handblown vases, elaborate ribbons, ceramic pots made locally, and blooming seasonal displays.

Her shop was an ode to Christmas, stuffed full and bursting with all the flowers and plants that filled people with Christmas joy.

She loved the nectarine and rose scent of amaryllis. The heady fullness of eucalyptus and the vanilla spice of a Christmas orchid. She couldn't help but laugh at the bright red pop of holly berries, smile at the hidden joy of running her fingers over a prickly pine cone, or feel a kindred warmth to the needles protecting the soft flesh of the Christmas cactus.

When she was inside For the Love of Flowers, surrounded by hundreds of blooms and wrapped in yards of garland and fairy lights, she couldn't help but feel hopeful. It was all the other moments of the day that left her feeling . . . hollow.

She kept up a happy façade for her family. Of course she did. For Louise, she took skating breaks, sledding trips, guzzled hot cocoa, and told her how her nana was their Christmas angel, watching over them and making sure their Christmas wishes came true.

It was Christmas. Or close enough. Only three days. The caravan of relatives arrived yesterday, and they'd already taken over everything. The cooking, the present-giving, the countless family activities. It was a blizzard of activity, which left Corey to do what she did best.

For the past five days, she'd been working from sunup until sunset at the Christmas Market. She and Elizabeth traded shifts at their booth. It was a clever setup—they had a mistletoe booth, kissing included, and more bouquets, wreaths, and plants carefully tended to bloom beautifully at Christmastime than anyone could possibly imagine.

When Corey wasn't at the booth she was in the shop, creating more Christmas arrangements, pricking her fingers on pine needles, and bending over wire cutters and evergreen boughs until her back hurt and her eyes crossed making dozens of handmade wreaths.

Sometimes, when it was late and she was still weaving spruce with gold ribbon and winterberry, her mind wandered. She'd find herself writing letters in her imagination.

Dear Lee, they always began. Dear Lee. From there, they'd take a thousand different turns—

I miss you.

Where are you?

Why haven't you come?

Louise started school this year. She wants to be a doctor when she grows up.

My mom is gone, I miss her. It's hard missing her so much.

Are you safe? Are you happy? Are you taking care of yourself?

Will you write me this Christmas?

I'm sorry I never told you what I wanted. You. I wanted you.

The letters in her imagination would always end the same. *Merry Christmas.*

Starting December 1st, she'd checked the mail three times a day. On December fifteenth, she moved to four times a day. Now, on December twenty-second, she'd already checked the mailbox three times. As if mail would come at any other time than eleven fifteen, which is when it always arrived. As if, somehow, after eleven fifteen, she'd magically get another letter.

But just like she couldn't help the beating of her heart, she couldn't help the hope and the wishing.

This Christmas.

This Christmas.

If . . . no, *when* Lee wrote, she'd tell him that she loved him. She'd ask him to come.

Corey looked around her little shop, overflowing with fragrant blossoms and gave a smile to the ball of mistletoe hanging over the door. Then she tugged another box full of Christmas bouquets and wreaths onto the sidewalk in front of For the Love of Flowers. The winter air nipped at her cheeks, but she was flushed and hot from loading crates full of flowers onto their little delivery sled and hauling wreaths back and forth between the shop and their Christmas Market booth.

"Is this it?" Elizabeth nodded at the box as Corey lifted it onto the wooden slats of the sled.

Elizabeth was decked out in elf ears, a little pointed green hat, and striped tights that matched her short green dress. She was having the time of her life charming couples into kissing under the mistletoe and then selling them the most beautiful Christmas arrangements they'd ever seen.

"For now." Corey eyed the sled, thinking that the wreaths and bouquets wouldn't last long. Today was the last day of the market and it seemed like the whole town had come out. Plus, her cousins and aunts and uncles had threatened to swing through and buy up everything at the booth. She knew they were good to their word.

"Who's at the booth now?" If Elizabeth wasn't there, then she may have put up a "closed" sign, or . . .

"Petunia."

They grinned at each other. Petunia was one of their favorite people in town. She came by nearly every week to grab a fresh bouquet of her namesake. Corey had always loved anyone over the age of eighty, but Petunia was in a class of her own.

"Erma's there too, so people are swarming the booth."

Corey smiled, a little wistfully. "I bet they are."

Probably they were hoping for a soulmate prediction for Christmas. Wouldn't that be something to tell for years to come? Miss Erma, the famed soulmate psychic, predicting their love match under the mistletoe.

"You alright?" Elizabeth took the handle of the sled, ready to tug it back along the snowy sidewalk to the market.

"I'm okay. Just thinking about . . . Christmas."

Elizabeth didn't question her. She was prickly and sarcastic, often spiky like the Christmas cactus, but she was also soft and caring.

"I'll watch the booth for the rest of the day. Take it down tonight. You take the night off."

"I couldn't—"

"Take the night off. Or we'll have problems."

Corey smiled. Nodded. Years into their partnership, she knew better than to argue when Elizabeth got that glint in her eyes.

As soon as Elizabeth saw that she'd conceded, she gave a jaunty elflike wave and then pulled her sled of flowers down the sidewalk.

Corey watched her for a minute, smiling at the pinch of cold, the scent of snow, and the sounds of Bing Crosby singing "I'll be Home for Christmas." She could smell the gingerbread and cinnamon drifting up the street from the market. She could feel the happiness in the air, sprinkled over the whole town, sticking to the snow like gold dust glitter on frosting.

Overhead, the winter blue sky was tinged with cottony strands of snow clouds, just waiting to blow a dusting of snow over the town.

Corey smiled and rubbed her arms. She was sweaty, sore, dressed in a red and green wool dress with a poinsettia pinned in her hair. She knew, from all the weeks past, that she had pine needles in her hair, rose and amaryllis petals stuck to her dress, and a bit of ribbon or twine or mistletoe tucked into her pocket.

The petals would fall off her at the end of the day when she undressed and then collapsed into bed. Or she'd find the pine needles on her pillowcase in the morning. She felt all dirty and rumpled, like she rolled around in a field of Christmas flowers every day.

Dear Lee, she began, looking out over Romeo, *if you could see me, you'd laugh. I'm covered in Christmas, from my head to my toes—*

She went inside her little shop, the warm, floral rich air surrounding her like a comforting hug. She'd clean up, close up, and then go find Louise who was currently making a gingerbread house with her Aunt Annabel and her cousins.

She promised herself that she'd only check the mailbox two or three more times today.

Dear Lee, Merry Christmas.

20

———————

Lee stood in front of For the Love of Flowers. In all his imaginings, he'd never imagined this. But it was perfect. It was the most perfect place he'd ever seen. Even if he hadn't known Corey started this shop, he would've felt her in it.

The shop was small, a fifteen-foot glass window at the front with the name of the shop scripted in frosted letters. There were evergreen garlands and holly berries hanging from the eaves, icicle lights glowing, and stands full of fir boughs, pine cones, red dogwood and gold trimmed ribbon. At the wooden front door, there was a strand of golden Christmas bells hanging from the brass handle.

His heart, he'd sworn it was already broken, but when he saw the small Christmas tree, crooked and scraggly, and weighed down with ornaments at the front door, his heart splintered all over again. There were red holly berries in the snow at his feet, and for a moment, he thought that he wouldn't be surprised if it were actually his heart's blood.

The window of the shop was slightly fogged, the inside so much warmer than the cold chill of the winter afternoon. But still, he could see a garden of red blossoms, of white frosted petals, pink and green, and silver and gold.

The inside of the shop was the Eden that Cordelia had always promised. There were Christmas lights strung from the ceiling and they bounced off and coated the flowers in a golden luminescence. Exactly like sunrise on Christmas morning.

For so many years, he'd thought about coming here, sitting with her, learning the language of her flowers. He wouldn't write her then. He could write her with a look, with the pads of his fingers brushing across her cheek, with a press of his hand in hers, with the offer of himself to her for the rest of their lives.

Lee stared down at the red berries scattered in the snow. He'd walked here in a sort of fugue, only knowing that even if Cordelia was gone, he needed to see someplace where she'd left a piece of herself. Something that was a part of her.

He'd realized as he passed the revelry of the Christmas Market, the laughter, the mitten-stealing reindeer, the hot cocoa and the merry making, that even if Cordelia was gone, she was still here.

There was a booth where two older women sold wreaths and flowers. A ball of mistletoe with a line of people. Hot cocoa and peppermint sticks. A table of kids decorating gingerbread houses. Lee wondered if one of them might be Louise, and he searched them each for green eyes, but then he was past them all. Ahead was the flower shop with all of Cordelia's dreams wrapped up in it.

On the way, Lee passed an elf on the sidewalk, pulling a sled of flowers and wreaths. She gave him an odd look, but Lee barely noticed. People often gave him odd looks since he'd lost his arm, but he'd stopped noticing years ago.

"Hey. Are you—"

He shook his head and waved, saying, "Merry Christmas," as he passed her by. He was entirely focused on the flowers crowding the sidewalk ahead.

Now he could see that inside there was a small woman with a long-handled broom, sweeping up. Her back was to him, and she was hidden by the strands of garland and the profusion of blooms, but he could tell she was petite and young. Maybe this was Elizabeth.

Lee didn't know what he'd say when he went inside. He only knew that he couldn't leave Romeo without seeing what Cordelia had made. Maybe he'd find a bouquet of roses and hibiscus, maybe he'd ask after Louise, make sure she had everything she needed, and if she didn't, then he'd help.

He stared at the door, and a flash of copper caught his eye. His heart thudded, and then he reached out and ran his finger over the cold metal of a penny set into the door's wooden frame.

"Good luck." He smiled as he pressed his finger to the cold metal.

Then he pulled open the door to the tinkle of Christmas bells.

Stepping inside was like entering another world. The heat hit him first. It felt tropical warm, lush and soothing.

All the blooming things perfumed the air with an intoxicating scent that beckoned him to stay, to dream, to be. There was the chest-aching scent of fir and cedar, the tropical floral notes of vanilla and spice, and the Christmas smells of cinnamon and rose blossoms.

Cordelia had been right. He was surrounded by a garden and all he wanted to do was stay. The woman called something from the back room, *be right there*, or *just a moment*. Her husky voice was muffled by the soft Christmas music, but it still brushed over him like a rose petal floating across his skin.

His breath was coming in short bursts and his hand was shaking. He was gripping the white box with the ornament and his letter so hard that his knuckles had turned white. He'd forgotten he'd been holding it.

There was a dreadful ache in his chest and his throat was scratchy and sore. Maybe it hadn't been a good idea to come here. There was a chair in the corner, hidden behind a potted Christmas tree and a bucket of long-stemmed red roses. It was a stuffed wingback chair with navy blue fabric and tiny gold stars and silver crescent moons. It was so hidden and out of the way that Lee knew immediately that it was for him. It was a little spot that Cordelia had carved into her garden just for him.

Next to the chair was a wrought-iron table with a bouquet of a dozen red roses and bloom after bloom of red hibiscus. On the table was a small wooden rose, the one he'd carved for her years ago.

He wanted to weep. It hurt so much he wanted to weep.

He dropped his chin and closed his eyes.

"Can I help you?"

It was the woman. She had a soft, husky voice, low

and gentle. It sounded to him like the kind of voice he'd be able to listen to for hours at a time. There was a soothing quality to it, one you didn't hear often. It felt, he realized, like the voice of someone who would never judge you and who would always understand you.

He turned slowly, scared to look at the woman because he didn't know what his expression would show or how he'd react to seeing anyone that had known Cordelia well.

He looked up slowly, clutching the gift in his hand.

"I . . ." He stopped.

The Christmas lights glowed, threading her auburn hair with golden light. She was petite, delicately boned, with the largest hazel—they'd always been hazel, hadn't they?—but no, they were the largest green eyes he'd ever seen. They drew him in, so much so that it was hard to notice anything else. The flush in her cheeks, the pine needles caught in her dress, the way she seemed strong, like an evergreen is strong, staying green and hopeful all year round, no matter what.

It was her.

He knew her.

She was the girl who had shared her chocolate yule log. The woman he'd made love to in New York, who left him when he'd been so sure that what he'd felt might've been love.

It was . . .

He stared at her. Took in every inch of her. He knew her. And it wasn't just . . . it wasn't just from those two meetings. It was something else.

It was the way she looked at him. It was the way his heart pounded and the way he wanted to cross the room and pull her against him and hold her tight. It was the feeling in the air, the one that pulsed and tingled and flowed between them, holding them both tight in its embrace.

Lee didn't know he was crying until he felt the hot wetness slide down his cheek. The salt pooled at the corner of his mouth, tasting hopeful, tasting like a Christmas star.

He was afraid to speak. What if he did, and the magic was broken? What if what he believed was a hope born out of desperation and grief?

Or what if . . . there really was a bit of Christmas magic left in this world?

She looked at him as if . . . as if she could read his heart, and she found the words beautiful.

"Corey?" His voice was rough, raw. But that wasn't only who she was, right? So he asked, praying with everything in him, "Cordelia?"

She trembled. Her whole body trembled like a tree shaking in a December wind. Her face flushed and she lifted a hand to press against her chest.

She stared at the box in his hand, the letter folded on top.

Then she looked at him, the world, a decade of love written between them, and whispered, "Lee?"

She *knew* him.

When he nodded, relief and shock, thick and urgent flooded him. Then Cordelia flung herself across the room and wrapped her arms around him. He held her and wept.

~

Cordelia

He was *Lee*.

Lee.

When Corey had seen him with his back turned, staring at the hibiscus and rose bouquet, a glossy shiver had run over her skin. Something had prodded her forward, whispering, *you know him*.

He was tall, wide-shouldered, with night-dark hair. She couldn't tell anything else from behind except . . . he made her pulse thrum with a vibrating melody that pulsed through her veins. She was dizzy and lightheaded with it.

Breathless.

When he turned, she couldn't bring herself to believe that the man in front of her was real. He was beautiful, a worn, sorrowful angel, roughened and care-warn, but so full of kindness and warmth that it practically lit him from the inside out.

He was in a red flannel, jeans, and leather boots—isn't that what he always wore?—and the tips of his ears and his nose were red from the cold. He was tanned brown from long days spent under the relentless sun, and there were small lines that creased from the corner of his eyes. People always say that the eyes are the mirror of the soul, and Corey believed it for the first time because in his eyes, she saw something she hadn't expected.

She saw her other half.

She saw starry nights and first snowfalls. Crescent moons and hands held across time and space. She saw brownies and sugar cookies and flowers pressed with care. She saw a man who loved, who gave, who cared.

In his hand, he held a gift, and on top, an envelope with her name scrawled across it. She knew his writing.

She would recognize it anywhere. But even without it, she would know him.

When he said her name, shock, relief, and love thick in his voice, she could only nod. When she said, *Lee*, and he nodded, she came undone and flew into his arms.

She buried herself against him, breathed in his pine and snowy night smell. Pressed her cheek to his heart, held her arms around his chest, recognized the shuddering and tears as a mirror of what she was feeling.

"You came." She pressed her lips to his heart. "I wanted you to come. I wrote and I prayed you would come. I wanted you to come so much. I kept wishing, I kept writing, I wanted you, why didn't you come sooner—"

He dug his hand through her hair. He'd dropped the gift when she ran into his arms, and now his fingers were roaming over her, pressing against her, pulling her close. She couldn't get close enough. Couldn't tell him everything she wanted to say.

"I thought you were gone. They said you died—"

"No, my mom, last year when I came to New York—"

"Cordelia—"

"I'm named after her. I didn't—"

"I thought I was too late. I wasted ten years. I wasted last year. I've wanted to tell you—"

"I love you." She pressed her mouth to his. She tasted the salt of tears, the joy of Christmas in hints of peppermint and icing-coated kisses.

He broke off and made a desperate sound. "You love me."

"I love you." She pressed another kiss to his mouth and burrowed her hands against the warmth of his flannel and heat of his abdomen. "For years. I've loved you—"

"Did you know? Did you know how much and how long I've loved you? Cordelia?" He opened his eyes and held her to him.

She knew that he never cried, that he hadn't in his whole life. Yet here he was, holding her against him, tears falling because it was Christmas . . . because they were finally where they were meant to be.

"I think, maybe I started to realize it, when you sent me flowers."

He kissed the edge of her mouth, then his hand paused on her cheek as if he only just realized what they'd been doing. Kissing. Touching. He held still.

She kept herself against him, pressing into his warmth, her face tilted toward him.

"Cordelia?" He whispered her name, almost as if he was afraid to speak it.

"Lee?"

It felt so good to say his name out loud.

She was a star, floating in the sky, glowing and luminous, a ball of energy waiting to flare bright and combust. Was she the North Star? Was he home?

"I came to ask, if you could love me, if you could want me in person, if you could want more than a Christmas letter once a year, if—"

She brushed her hands across his cheeks, felt the cool stubble on his jaw, and the smoothness of his skin. Her heart throbbed in her chest. He was here. Her Lee.

But it was better than that. Even better than just her Lee.

He was Louise's too.

He always had been.

"If?" she whispered, pressing a soft kiss to his lips.

He pulled her close and held her tight against him. They were in the center of a universe of flowers with all the Christmas blossoms around them. They were wrapped in garland, sparkling under Christmas lights, perfumed by red roses and amaryllis.

She'd never imagined this. She couldn't have imagined anything so wonderful.

"I can't find the words." Lee stared down at her, his voice rough. "It was you." She knew he meant that it was her all along, but also, that it was her in New York. That their entire lives had been two hearts intersecting. "I always said I didn't have a home. But you were my home. I said I didn't have a family. But you were my family. I said I could never love. But you were always my love. Even when I didn't have the words, they were still there between us. Cordelia, I . . . I love you as if I'm taking my last breath and you are the only one I want to see there beside me when I finally exhale."

She held him closer, pressed her hand over his, holding his trembling fingers close.

Then she put her lips to every sparkling tear on his cheeks, kissing them away.

"You were Chris," she says, wondering.

"When we first met?"

She nodded.

"It's what Freddy called me, and he called himself Nick."

"But the next time, in New York . . ." She'd called him Chris that night too.

"I told you my name was Lee in the bar. Didn't you . . . ?"

"No. I couldn't hear you." A warmth spread through her, filling her with a languid, floating heat.

"Cordelia?" His thumb ran over her cheek, and she realized suddenly that he was wiping away her tears too. "Corey?"

He was asking if she was okay, if this was alright, if . . . if . . .

"What do you want? I'll do whatever you want." He paused and waited for her answer, his body comforting hers, the feel of him wrapping around her.

He was so familiar to her. Everything about him. Standing in his arms was like holding his letter in her hands, wrapping herself in his words, only better. A thousand times better. It was the difference between looking at a map of the stars and lying underneath a meteor shower.

"I want you." She pressed another kiss to him and held him tight. "I want you to stay for Christmas. I want you to stay for . . . for your birthday and for Valentine's and then for my birthday and then . . . Lee?"

He watched her with the same yearning that was spreading through her. "Yes."

She smiled. She didn't know if he was telling her he'd stay or if he was answering her saying his name. But she had something more to tell him.

"You have a family."

He nodded. His grip tightened on her. "I know."

She shook her head. "No. Lee. You have a family. Me and Louise. That night in New York. You and me? We made a baby. We made Louise. You're her dad. You're—"

Lee pulled her to him, and whatever fear she had fell away, melted like ice in the sun.

He said her name, over and over, and then he was

kissing her, and she kissed him back. A family, he whispered, and there was so much reverence, so much awe and love in his voice, that she could only hang onto him and kiss him as he told her how much he loved her.

She left him for a moment. Turned the closed sign. Locked the door. Closed the blinds. Turned off the lights.

The shop became a bower of fragrant flowers, mistletoe and evergreen, Christmas lights and rose petals. Corey looked at Lee standing in the center of a floral paradise.

He was smiling at her, his dark eyes full of every love word he'd ever written and everything he wanted to tell her now. He once said that he looked older and meaner than he was. But that wasn't right at all. He looked like her best friend, the keeper of her heart, the one who was meant to be with her for the whole of this life.

Once he'd said he didn't know if he could come back to the world, he thought maybe he was too broken. And she'd told him that she would let the flowers heal him. And she'd let the flowers say all the things that couldn't be said.

So as she walked toward him, a promise in her gaze, she lifted her dress over her head and let it pool on the tile floor.

Lee let out a shuddering breath and whispered her name. That reverent whisper coated her skin with a shimmery warmth.

She kicked off her shoes and then pulled her tights down her thighs and calves. They ran over her skin, the soft wool warmth giving way to the humid, fragrant heat of the shop. She was in underwear and a bra now. Lee's chest was rising and falling in a rapid staccato.

There was an ache inside her. She wanted to hold him. Kiss him. Love him.

As she stepped closer she pulled a dozen red roses free and scattered their petals on the floor. "For love."

He watched the petals fall at their feet.

She plucked white narcissus free and let each petal fall through her fingers like snowdrops spinning to earth. "For new beginnings."

A smile tugged at the corner of Lee's lips as he watched her scatter the leaves of mistletoe. "For romance."

Finally, she let red hibiscus fall from her fingers.

Lee watched her, his gaze burning as bright as any candle.

"For passion, for friendship, for love."

The Christmas lights glowed bright between them. The flowers and their meanings filled the air.

She stepped close to Lee and pressed her lips to his. He closed his eyes and breathed her in.

And then she pulled him to the ground. Soon they were both bare, skin to skin. Everywhere they touched, they moved together. The petals crushed beneath them, coating them with sticky scents and filling the air with perfume. They curved around each other, touching, and kissing, and loving. Until touching wasn't enough, and kissing wasn't enough.

Lee pressed his mouth to Cordelia's. He settled against her and she arched up to him. Their bodies were slick with sweat, and the feel of him made her insides sing.

"I've already loved you forever. Let me . . ." Lee looked down at her and brushed her hair from her face. "Let me love you forever and a day. Let me tell you that I love you for every day for the rest of our lives. Cordelia? Please?"

She reached up and threaded her hands through his thick hair. Pulled his mouth down to hers. "Forever and a day."

He was inside her then, filling her and loving her. He brushed his mouth over her, gently sometimes and then desperately others, his fingers brushed her cheeks, caressed her, and circled in insistent strokes over her so that as he loved her, she climbed higher and higher until she was shattering around him and he was holding her tight, gasping and loving, and then losing himself in her so that he could only follow her shining light into the oblivion.

He collapsed to the floor, crushing more petals, and then pulled her into his side. His breathing was heavy, and her heart pounded wildly. He stroked his hand over her chest, pressed his palm to her heart.

"Thank you." He whispered this, his voice raw as he circled his hand over her heart.

Corey smiled at the love in his voice.

"Merry Christmas, Lee."

He made a happy sound and pressed his lips to her neck. "Merry Christmas, Cordelia."

She loved those words. Loved them.

There wasn't anything more magical in the whole world.

Christmas Day

21

Lee

Lee had never imagined that in coming to Romeo, he'd gain a hundred and three relatives overnight and a town full of people who took him in as their own as soon as they met him. But that was what happened, and if it felt like a Christmas miracle, then he supposed that was what it was.

For the last few days he'd been thrown into every Hobday Christmas tradition celebrated for the last one hundred and fifty years. Sledding, gingerbread baking, snowman making. Burning dinners and doing dishes, lying under the lights of the Christmas tree and singing carols badly.

Corey showed him all the places she'd written about. The nooks and crannies of her shop, the cozy apartment upstairs, the skating pond, the tilting Victorian, the guest room with the ugly paisley wallpaper, her bedpost where his heart ornament had hung, the utility sink in the basement laundry room.

Lee had never felt at home anywhere until now.

Louise met him the morning after he arrived since Corey had texted her sister and asked if Louise could spend the night at her place. When she arrived back home, with her backpack and a small stuffed frog in her arms, she took him in with a wide, steady gaze and then asked, "Are you my dad?"

He knelt in front of her. Corey stood behind him, her hand pressed to his shoulder. "I am."

He didn't know how she'd known, but sometimes kids were able to know things that adults were blind to.

She watched him solemnly, taking in her mom standing behind him with her hand on his arm, his black hair, the same shade as hers, and the hopeful smile on his face.

"How come you weren't here before?" She tilted her head and held her backpack and stuffed frog closer to her chest.

There was a raw ache in his throat when he answered. "I got lost, and I couldn't find my way home."

She nodded as if this made perfect sense. "But you're here now."

"I'm here now."

She reached out then and touched his arm. "What's this?"

"A prosthetic."

"Does it hurt?"

"No."

"Do you like it?"

"Yes. It helps me."

She thought about this, then said, "Will you go sledding with me? And then make me hot cocoa? Do you have a present for me for Christmas? Are you going to live with us? DeeDee said I didn't have a dad, but I always told her I did. Do you like candy canes?"

He was lucky that he was kneeling because if he hadn't been, he might've fallen over from the amount of love that washed over him at her easy acceptance and her complete faith in him.

Later that night, she gave him a piece of yellow construction paper with a drawing on it. There was the flower shop, their home on top, and the three of them next to a Christmas tree. It was a map, she'd said, in case he got lost again. He promised that he'd keep it forever.

For the last three days, he and Corey touched constantly. They held hands, wrapped arms around each other, leaned into each other's sides, sat with thighs pressed together, and kissed and held each other tight. It was as if they were making up for ten years of not touching and not kissing and not loving.

Even now, on Christmas night, while everyone else was outside making snow angels on the freshly fallen snow, preparing for the family candle lighting, Lee held Cordelia in his lap on the rug next to the Christmas tree. He breathed in the floral scent of her and pressed a kiss to the line of her jaw. She leaned back against his chest and held his hand to her heart.

The Christmas presents were all unwrapped, little bits of ribbon and stray paper still lined the floor. Pine needles stuck out of the rug and the tree smelled like a winter forest and warm sap. The fire crackled and popped, letting off a toasty heat and a sweet, woodsy smell. For as ugly as the tree was, it was beautiful too. It was crooked, drooping with decades of ornaments, and swathed in strands of cranberries and popcorn. The Christmas lights winked at them like stars in the sky.

Lee was warm, happy, and loved. He felt Cordelia's heart beating beneath his hand and felt grateful, so grateful for the Christmas that she decided to write him back.

He pressed another kiss to her lips. "I have a Christmas card for you."

"You do?"

They'd already exchanged gifts. He gave her the ornament he'd made and the letter he'd written her. He went shopping in Romeo and bought her presents of books and gourmet chocolate and dance lessons for two at the studio and a gold necklace with rubies in the shape of a rose. He found Louise a bike with streamers, a lizard stuffed animal to be friends with her frog, and all the books she said she needed to figure out how to be a doctor.

Louise gave him a gift that she'd wrapped herself. It was a flowerpot she'd painted bright red and green. She told him they'd plant daffodil bulbs in it and in the spring they'd get to see them bloom. Lee couldn't speak his throat was so tight, so instead he pulled his daughter close and gave her a hug.

Corey gave him a freezer full of brownies and a fruitcake she made just for him. She found him a special edition of *The Hobbit* and took him to the community theatre to watch *The Nutcracker*. She went to the coffee roaster and had them make a special blend just for him.

She made him a home and asked him to stay.

And now, he had one more gift for her.

He took the small card from his pocket. It was tiny, only a scrap of gold foil with paper pasted on the back. The gold patina caught and reflected the shine of the Christmas lights. His hand shook as he pressed the card into Corey's hand.

Corey looked down at the gold foil and the lights flickering off the smooth surface. "Is this . . .?" She rubbed her thumb over the gold and leaned back into him. "You kept this."

"From the chocolate yule log." The one they'd shared.

A smile pulled at the corners of her mouth as she tilted her head to look up at him. He moved his fingers over the edges of her smile, and she pressed a kiss to his seeking fingers.

"I practically fell in love with you that night. I had an obsession with chocolate yule logs for years after that."

She laughed and shook her head. The highlights of her auburn hair gleamed in the firelight. "The second I saw you, I thought it was love at first sight."

"It couldn't have been." He smiled at the warmth of having her in his lap. He'd never get over being able to hold her, to seeing her look at him with so much love.

"Why not?"

"Because you loved me before you saw me. It was love before first sight."

She made a small noise, a happy one full of agreement, but then she tapped him on his chest. "How do you know?"

"Because it was the same for me. Flip it over." He nodded at the gold foil card.

She didn't do what he asked right away. Instead, they

stared at each other, reliving what they'd done that morning while the sky was dark, and the snow was falling, and they were cocooned under down blankets and warm flannel sheets. Afterward, they'd made hot cocoa and coffee and kissed until the morning light shone through the frost-covered window and painted the bedroom in golden hues.

Finally, Corey's cheeks tinted pink and Lee resisted the urge to forget about the Christmas card, the candle lighting, and everything else to instead go upstairs and find that paisley wallpapered bedroom and some mistletoe.

Instead he pulled Corey closer, brushed a kiss over her lips, and then watched her slowly turn the Christmas card over.

Her head was bent as she read what he'd written. A warmth flowed between them, a tug and pull that had kept them together for a decade. There was a light burning inside him and it filled the room as he watched her mouth turn up at the corners.

Then she read his letter out loud.

"Dear Cordelia. Will you marry me this Christmas? Lee."

Her bottom lip trembled, and she blinked quickly as she looked up at him. "Do you have a pen?"

He nodded and pulled a pen from his pocket.

She uncapped it, dropped the cap to the rug next to stray pine needles and then set the paper on her folded knees. This was one of those times—again—where their letter would be wobbly and written on top of knees.

Lee watched as Corey slowly formed her letters. Her unguarded u's, her trusting l's, the loop of the y that he loved so much. She handed him the card with her answer.

Dear Lee,

Yes.

Yours,
Cordelia

In the darkest part of the night, when the only light was the moon and the stars shining overhead, Lee stood in the snowy front yard with Cordelia, Louise, and all the Hobdays from far and wide. They each held a white candle, ready to pass a light from one person to the next.

Cordelia watched him with pink cheeks, a happy, glowing expression and so much love. Louise was bundled in a snowsuit next to him, holding her candle aloft as if she didn't dare to drop it.

When Cordelia leaned forward, passing on the light to him, she whispered, "I have another gift."

"How? I don't need anything else."

She smiled as her flame caught and lit his candle. The two of them combined and burned bright.

"The phone call I just had? It was about your brother. He's been looking for you for years. When you came here, somehow, someone knew about him, and he's . . . Lee, he's on his way. Here. To Romeo. You're finally going to see your brother again."

Lee stared at Cordelia. Unable to comprehend that in one Christmas he'd gained a family, a home, and now, a brother too. He'd once given away the ornament his brother had given him because he thought all his Christmas magic had been used up. But now he knew there was no limit, no end to what Christmas could do.

"Now me! Dad, light my candle!" Louise stood on her tiptoes and held out her candle to him.

Corey gave him a wide smile, and then he turned and passed on the glowing light. Soon, the whole night was burning bright with the flickering glow of candlelight.

"Merry Christmas, Lee."

I love you, she was saying, *I love you with my whole heart*. So he said it right back.

"Merry Christmas, Cordelia. Merry Christmas."

one year later

22

Cordelia Weston
  1701 Main Street
  Romeo, NY

Dear Cordelia,

Merry Christmas. Did I mention how much I love your brownies? If you ever decide to stop making them, I think my world will come to an end. I'm sorry for jaywalking yesterday on my way to grab a coffee from The SweetStop, but as you know, those who love fruitcake can't help but jaywalk. In my defense, I was in a hurry because Louise wanted a slice of chocolate yule log for dessert, and I didn't want to disappoint her.

By the way, did you see how she made her Uncle Gabe lose his appetite when she decorated all her gingerbread men with pink frosting squiggled in the shape of intestines and brains from her anatomy picture books? I've never laughed so hard in my life. She was surprisingly accurate. He swears she'll follow in the Cavanaugh family footsteps, but I doubt it, I think she's set on becoming a doctor.

I wish I could tell you how wonderful the past year has been. How I finally met the woman I've loved for most of my life, how I have a daughter who I'd do anything for, how I'm finally home.

All those years I was searching, Cordelia, it was right here all along. I wish I could get the words right to tell you. But it's Christmas, and I thought you might like to know . . . I'm happy. I'm so happy that it fills every inch of me, every breath and every word.

It's Christmas Eve today. I'll describe it to you, so you can be here with me.

I'm in my home, and right now, it smells like gingerbread and hot chocolate. I'm sitting at the kitchen counter, writing you. Outside, the sky is dark and the streetlamps glow a yellow gold. Snowflakes sparkle silver in the light as they tumble down to the sidewalk. It's cold outside, there's frost on the window, but here in the kitchen it's toasty and warm. Below us, there's a flower shop, and sometimes I can smell roses or lilacs, or evergreen, but today, there's only chocolate and cinnamon and clove.

There's gingerbread baking in the oven and a bowl of frosting on the counter. My daughter, she's the one with the long black hair and the serious expression, don't let her fool you, she's already swiped at least three globs of frosting from the bowl. I pretend not to notice, but on the third swipe I look up and wink at her. She giggles and runs away, her frosting coated finger in her mouth.

There's Christmas music playing, my favorite song, "Silent Night," and another, "I'll be Home for Christmas." Sometimes I add in my wife's favorite song, "Don't go Breaking My Heart," just to hear her laugh. And sometimes when she laughs, I sweep her up and spin her around the kitchen until she's dizzy so that she falls against me, and I can steal as many kisses as I want.

There. Now you know my secret.

Here's another since I always promised to tell all my truths to you. I'm in love. Desperately. My wife, she's at the Christmas tree, hanging the ornaments I made this year. It's an ugly tree, truly hideous, but it's wrapped in swathes of roses and hibiscus, and crowned with handmade ornaments, so, well, maybe it's actually the most beautiful Christmas tree I've ever seen.

Or maybe that's my wife. She's glowing. Her hair shines in the Christmas lights, her cheeks are pink, she's humming along with the music, and when she looks over at me, she smiles. Cordelia, do you know how her smile makes me feel? It makes me feel like I'm home. Like it's Christmas morning, and a candle is burning, just for me, and I'm home.

And, well, you're coming over, walking this way, you have a ball of mistletoe in your hands, and that particular smile on your face that I really, truly love. So I'll have to end this letter, because I'm going to kiss you. I'm going to kiss you and tell you Merry Christmas.

And then, I'll give you my love.

Merry Christmas, Cordelia.

—Lee

~

Dear Lee,

Let's not stay up too late putting together Louise's gifts. I have a bedroom full of rose petals and a Christmas gift just for you. Before we're overrun by family tomorrow, I'd like a bit of you for myself.

Do you remember, a long time ago, when you asked me whether I thought things would get better or if they'd just get different?

I have another answer. They keep getting better.

When you're here and I'm with you, the world can only keep getting better. Every day with you is the best day of my life.

Thank you for being my heart.

Merry Christmas, my love.

Yours,
    Cordelia

Merry Christmas

JOIN SARAH READY'S NEWSLETTER

Want more *Dear Christmas*? Get an exclusive bonus epilogue!

When you join the Sarah Ready Newsletter you get access to sneak peaks, insider updates, exclusive bonus scenes and more.

Join today for an exclusive epilogue:

www.sarahready.com/newsletter

ABOUT THE AUTHOR

Award-winning author Sarah Ready writes women's fiction, contemporary romance and romantic comedy.

Sarah writes stand-alone romances, including *Josh and Gemma Make a Baby*, *Josh and Gemma the Second Time Around*, *French Holiday*, *The Space Between*, *Ghosted*, *Switched*, and romcoms in the Soul Mates in Romeo series, all of which can be found at her website: www.sarahready.com.

She lives in a house by the beach on a small Caribbean island with her family and her water-loving pup.

You can learn more and find upcoming titles at: www.sarahready.com.

Stay up to date, get exclusive epilogues and bonus content. Join Sarah's newsletter at www.sarahready.com/newsletter.

ALSO BY SARAH READY

Stand Alone Romances:

The Fall in Love Checklist

Hero Ever After

Once Upon an Island

French Holiday

The Space Between

The Ghosted Series:

Ghosted

Switched

Josh and Gemma:

Josh and Gemma Make a Baby

Josh and Gemma the Second Time Around

Soul Mates in Romeo Romance Series:

Chasing Romeo

Love Not at First Sight

Romance by the Book

Love, Artifacts, and You

Married by Sunday

My Better Life

Scrooging Christmas